You'll never get enough of these cowboys!

Bestselling Harlequin Blaze author Debbi Rawlins makes all your cowboy dreams come true with her popular miniseries

Made in Montana.

The little town of Blackfoot Falls isn't so sleepy anymore...

In fact, it seems everyone's staying up late!

Get your hands on a hot cowboy with

#892 *Come Closer, Cowboy*

(May 2016)

#905 *Wild for You*

(August 2016)

#917 *Hot Winter Nights*

(November 2016)

And remember, the sexiest cowboys are Made in Montana!

Dear Reader,

Yes, we're still here in Blackfoot Falls, which is growing like crazy...unlike the small rural town where I've been living for the past ten years. We still have only one vet, and since I have a lot of animals, I know him pretty well.

Last year one of my pooches got into some mischief that required a visit to the doc. While I dialed the office, hoping and praying that the vet (whom I'll call John) would be there and wasn't making *ranch calls*, I got the idea for this book.

Now, John has a certain hobby that makes me a little crazy. To my mind, it's too risky for a forty-year-old part-timer. I'm not a pessimist by nature, but he is the only vet for seventy miles. And I trust him completely. What if he was put out of commission?

To occupy myself while I waited for my dog, I came up with Spencer, the hero in this book. After I paid the bill and they resuscitated me, I asked John a bunch of questions to help me develop the character. And then I lectured him on taking unnecessary risks. He just laughed and ignored me. He's married, so he's got that down to a science.

Hope you enjoy the story!

All my best,

Debbi Rawlins

Debbi Rawlins

Wild for You

ISBN-13: 978-0-373-79909-1

Wild for You

This edition published by arrangement with Harlequin Books S.A.

For questions and comments about the quality of this book, please contact us at CustomerService@Harlequin.com.

Printed in U.S.A.

Debbi Rawlins grew up in the country and loved Western movies and books. Her first crush was on a cowboy—okay, he was an actor in the role of a cowboy, but she was only eleven, so it counts. It was Houston, Texas, where she first started writing for Harlequin, and now she has her own ranch...of sorts. Instead of horses, she has four dogs, four cats, a trio of goats and free-range cattle on a few acres in gorgeous rural Utah.

Books by Debbi Rawlins

Harlequin Blaze

Made in Montana

Barefoot Blue Jean Night
Own the Night
On a Snowy Christmas Night
You're Still the One
No One Needs to Know
From This Moment On
Alone with You
Need You Now
Behind Closed Doors
Anywhere with You
Come On Over
This Kiss
Come Closer, Cowboy

To get the inside scoop on Harlequin Blaze and its talented writers, be sure to check out BlazeAuthors.com.

All backlist available in ebook format.

Visit the Author Profile page at Harlequin.com for more titles.

1

ERIN MURPHY TURNED onto Main Street and nearly had heart failure. How could a small, isolated Montana town have changed so much in three months? Blackfoot Falls didn't have a single traffic light, but the new steak house's flashing pink neon sign could probably be seen from Mars. Early-bird specials written with black marker on colored paper covered half the window. But she could live with those, misspellings and all. They lent to the charm of the quirky town.

She drove past the newly opened motel that had been under construction when she'd first discovered Blackfoot Falls. Erin would've preferred the modern building wasn't there, but she had taken it into consideration when she'd made a deal with the mayor, so no sweat on that front.

A small bakery now occupied a formerly empty storefront. Nothing flashy, so that wasn't too bad. Next to it, the Full Moon Saloon was new, too, but it had a cool vibe to it that could probably work in her favor.

Maybe.

Whatever.

She'd make it work. She had to.

The whole reason Erin had returned was to fix something she'd failed to do the first time around. Now she had another problem to solve…before the director had a stroke.

The independent film for which she'd been scouting locations was on a tight budget. She'd counted on those buildings being empty. It was a lot cheaper to stage than change.

All she could do for the moment was breathe. And hope the mayor had made allowances for the deal she'd made with Erin before leasing out the buildings. Sadie Thompson was a reasonable woman who'd understood that the group's pockets weren't deep, and a modest fee was better than nothing. Quite a few scenes would be shot around the quaint little town, later, in December.

Luckily, Erin made it to the other end of Main Street without encountering any more surprises. She checked into The Boarding House Inn with its restored turn-of-the-century rooms and interesting woodwork. Thank God nothing had changed since her last visit.

She dumped her duffel bag in the narrow closet and sent off a few texts. Thirty minutes ago she'd been looking forward to a much-needed nap. Now she wondered if it would be better to go snap some pictures of the new storefronts and send them to the director right away. Jason would pitch a fit no matter what, but at least she'd be giving herself more time to smooth things over.

On the other hand, she wouldn't be at her best, being this sleep deprived. She stared out the window and tried to relax. She smiled, though, seeing the cheesy Halloween decorations on some of the buildings.

Her cell rang, and it was Lila, of course. Even though Erin had just texted her friend that they'd talk later.

"So, you're in Blackfoot Falls. That was fast," Lila said. "When are you going to see him?"

Erin knew *him* meant Spencer Hunt, the reclusive, unreasonable, ill-tempered rancher who had thrown her off his property the last time she was here. He was also hot as hell. But Erin had never let a man's looks excuse him for being a jerk.

"This afternoon." Erin yawned. "After I take a nap."

Lila snorted. "We've been best friends since third grade. You think I can't tell when you're faking a yawn? You just don't want me coaching you on how to approach Mr. Tall, Dark and Mysterious."

"For one thing, coaching and butting in are not synonymous, and second, you're losing your touch because that yawn was real. I left Wyoming at 4:00 this morning."

"I was up early myself. We were shooting by 5:15 and freezing our behinds." Lila lowered her voice. "Jason's on a tear, cussing out everyone within hearing distance. Nothing's going right. The film is now officially over budget, and half the crew is ready to mutiny."

"So everything's normal."

"Pretty much."

Erin rubbed her tired eyes, glad she could still find some humor in the situation. "Well, I guess that settles it. I have another small snafu and was trying to decide when to tell Jason."

"Oh, no."

"It's not that big a deal, but it could cost a few bucks."

"Yeah, now isn't the time to bring it up."

Erin sighed. "I need to do more digging first."

They both had a lot riding on the indie film. So did Jason Littleton and two other friends, who'd thrown in their savings and were working their asses off for practically no money, all in the hope their modern Western would get noticed and launch their careers.

Erin and Lila had met the gang in film school, all of them full of dreams and plans to conquer Hollywood. For six years, Erin had willingly tackled every industry-related job that came her way. Like playing location scout and convincing people to allow footage to be shot on their land, sometimes in their homes.

She negotiated the fees, drew up contracts and arranged for the permits and insurance. She'd even chauffeured big shots from major studios and picked up their laundry. Just waiting to get her foot in the door. Because what she wanted more than anything was to make her own movies.

"Have you been listening at all?" Lila asked.

"Nope. Is it important? Because I seriously have to grab some sleep."

"Look, you need to listen to me. Jason really has his heart set on filming the final shoot-out on that mountain your guy owns. He'll forgive just about anything else but that. So if I were—"

"Screw Jason. I gave him two alternate locations. Really good ones. If Hunt doesn't want us on his property, there's not a damn thing I can do about it."

Lila waited a moment, then said, "You're the most persistent, driven, goal-oriented person I know. You'll convince him. But since you already know he's not motivated by money—"

Erin groaned. "Don't say it."

"It won't kill you to wear some makeup. Maybe do something with your hair."

"I asked you nicely…"

"And for heaven's sake, don't wear that big, stupid *Doctor Who* T-shirt."

Erin glanced down. "Which one?"

"Come on, Erin. Just treat it like a role you're playing. Smile. Be charming."

"You're the one who wants to be an actress, not me."

"I'm just saying…" Lila paused when someone called for her, but returned quickly. "We've both done some crappy jobs to get this far. Using a little sex appeal won't kill you. As for Jason…he isn't behaving any worse than most directors."

"Yeah, and we've always said we wouldn't be like those jerks."

"I know." Lila sighed. "It just feels like we're really close this time."

"We are," Erin said. "I feel it, too."

Lila chuckled. "You always do. The eternal optimist. I wish I could be more like you. I really do."

"You, my friend, are perfect just as you are."

"But not pretty enough to nab a decent role."

"Come on, Lila. You just said we're close." Erin didn't like her friend's resigned tone. She was just tired. Everyone on location was living out of suitcases and in drafty trailers with lousy beds. "We're going to kill it, and for the sequel, I'll get the assistant director's slot and you'll get a supporting actress role."

"Fingers and toes crossed," she said. "They're calling me. I have to go. You still have the list I gave you, right? And the makeup and heels?"

"Yep." Erin shook her head. She was the wrong person to convince Spencer Hunt to change his mind. Lila should be here instead of doing hair and makeup for that prissy Penelope Lane, who was playing the lead role.

Natural blonde Lila was gorgeous. Anywhere outside of Hollywood, she was an easy ten. And with his dark hazel eyes and his perfectly chiseled jaw, so was

Spencer Hunt. Still, Erin would've liked to see him try to say no to Lila.

Sighing, Erin found the checklist along with the bag of her friend's good intentions, dumped the contents on the bathroom counter and shuddered. Lots of stuff she didn't recognize. Good thing Lila had included what to wear and makeup instructions on the list. But adding a reminder for Erin to be charming… Really?

Oh, Jesus.

She thought again about Spencer and swallowed. He was going to laugh at her. Or worse, think she was pitiful. But if pity got him to sign on the dotted line, she could live with that.

DUSTY POKED HIS HEAD into the barn. "You expecting company?"

Spencer looked up from the vaccinations he'd laid out for the twin colts. He'd lived outside Blackfoot Falls for ten months now and barely knew a dozen people. His choice. Against his objections, Dusty had followed him from Boise, but the main reason Spencer had hired the kid was so he could avoid going into town. It hadn't stopped the nosy questions on the few occasions Spencer had picked up supplies himself, but he'd learned to deal with those.

"Nah, I didn't think so," Dusty said without waiting for a response. "I'll take care of whoever it is."

He turned back toward the road, then stopped, squinting hard and scratching his blond head.

"Problem?" Spencer asked.

"That lady from Hollywood drove a weird turquoise-colored car, didn't she?"

Erin Murphy was back? How long had it been?

Two…three months? Spencer strolled over to have a look for himself.

"Folks in town have been buzzing about that movie they're gonna start filming soon," Dusty said. "But no one said anything about her coming back."

"Her name's Erin."

At the sound of his voice Dusty jumped. "You might wanna step back some so she can't see you."

Spencer shook his head. "You finish pitching hay. I'll talk to her."

"You sure about that?" Dusty looked disappointed. "I don't mind telling her you aren't here," he said, pushing a hand through his shaggy hair, trying to tidy it up.

He'd been taken with Erin on her first visit and assumed she was an actress. She'd laughed at the idea, implied she wasn't pretty enough. When Dusty had asked what was wrong with those guys in California, Erin had blushed and changed the subject.

Spencer had thought about the spunky brunette a few times since that day. He couldn't say why for sure. The simple and most logical explanation was the lack of sex in his new life. Even though his eleven-month dry spell was self-imposed, he missed the warm soft body of a woman beside him. Not enough to give up his privacy. But maybe it was time to take an overnight trip out of town. Not to Idaho. He had no plans to return home anytime soon. If ever.

If not for last night's hard rain packing the dirt road, her tires would've been kicking up dust. But it was easy to see the odd-colored car. He knew for sure it was Erin before she turned onto the gravel driveway and veered left to avoid a mud puddle. He'd meant to fill in holes and grade the drive before the snow came.

"Do you think she'd go out with me?" Dusty asked. He hadn't moved, and Spencer hadn't noticed until now.

"You're nineteen," Spencer said, hiding his surprise. "She must have ten years on you."

"Things like age don't matter nowadays. And she doesn't act like one of those stuck-up Hollywood types, or I wouldn't even think about asking." Dusty dragged his gaze away from the car and studied Spencer. "I didn't think you were interested."

"I'm not. Ask her if you want." Spencer almost added that he shouldn't get his hopes up, but, hell, the kid technically was an adult. He just seemed young.

Spencer had no room to judge. His own immature arrogance had torn him from everything he'd loved and put him right here in this isolated little corner of Montana. And he'd been thirty-two at the time. No, he wasn't about to make the mistake of getting in Dusty's way.

They watched her park closer to the house and the stone walkway that led to the front door. Spencer didn't think she'd spotted them. She was too busy doing something in her car.

He grabbed his hat off the worktable. No sense waiting for her to come to him. He figured he knew what she wanted, and the answer was still no. She didn't even have to get out of the car.

"Hey, wait," Dusty said. "You're not gonna chase her off again, are ya?"

"If I have to." He heard the kid muttering something, but Spencer kept walking. Sure, he'd admit he wasn't unhappy to see her. But he prized his privacy and solitude above everything else. That wouldn't change.

She opened her door, swung two long bare legs out and planted a pair of red high heels on the ground.

Spencer's heart lurched in his chest and somehow

cut off his supply of oxygen. Anatomically that was impossible. He knew that better than most people. But that knowledge didn't put his equilibrium back to rights.

Stopping a few yards away from the car, he folded his arms across his chest and watched her stand. Her short denim skirt hit her just about midthigh. What he wouldn't give to take a nice, leisurely look, but as it was, he couldn't even swear the woman was Erin. His gaze hadn't made it up to her face yet.

After a brief glance at her close-fitting red sweater, his gaze lingered on her mouth, on the row of straight white teeth biting into the plump flesh of her bottom lip.

He seemed to recall that her eyes were brown. But he couldn't see them with her lashes lowered, head bent, her long dark hair falling forward and hiding half her face. She seemed more interested in the soft ground than in him. Wise move. If she wasn't careful, she'd get those skinny heels stuck in the mud.

"Erin?"

She glanced up. Smiled. "Mr. Hunt," she said, hanging on to the car door when she wobbled. "Hello. Nice to see you again."

"I can't imagine why you drove all the way out here," he said. "We have nothing to talk about."

"Well, I must admit..." She tilted her head slightly to the side, her smile changing to something sultrier. "I was hoping you'd changed your mind."

Tensing when she took another shaky step, he lowered his arms to his sides. "The only reason I came out here was to save you the trouble of getting out of your car." He glanced pointedly at her feet.

"Yeah, I never should have worn these heels out here. But I have an appointment right after this, so..." She gave a slight shrug, the pull of the sweater drawing his attention to the swell of her breasts.

He couldn't let that distract him. "Then you might as well be on your way," he said and watched her smile slip. It came right back, though.

She didn't just look different; she sounded different. Her sigh was soft, not filled with impatience and frustration like it had been when he'd first turned down her request to film on his land. And if she'd worn makeup before, she'd applied it with a much lighter touch. While she hadn't gone overboard, her high cheekbones appeared more prominent, and there was a slight sheen to her lips.

Looking past him, her smile widened suddenly. "Hi, Dusty," she called out with a wave, still clutching the car door.

When she took an unexpected step forward, Spencer automatically offered his hand.

She blinked at it and then was about to accept his help but said, "Wait." She turned around and reached for something inside the car.

The way she bent across the seat made Spencer think she wasn't used to wearing skirts. He told himself not to look, but he did. Only for a second before he turned his head. He hoped Dusty hadn't seen his brief moment of indiscretion. Spencer didn't care for the fact that the kid considered him a mentor, but how he felt about it didn't change anything.

Erin backed up and stood with a folder in her hand.

Probably a contract. Wouldn't happen.

He shook his head, tempted to let her fend for herself if she insisted on being stubborn. But good manners ingrained from the minute he learned to talk wouldn't allow it.

Again, he offered his hand, and she didn't hesitate to take it. Her palm was smooth and soft but not as silky as most of the women he knew back in Boise.

"You couldn't have picked a worse place to park," he said, trying to ignore the sweet scent of her skin.

"I see that." She took another step, her fingers curling around his knuckles. Her hand was small, but she had a strong grip.

Spencer took a shallow breath. "Look, why don't you get back in the car and—"

Erin gasped.

She pitched forward, digging her nails into his wrist.

He looked down and saw that her left heel had sunk deep into the rain-soaked dirt. She tried pulling it free but only managed to step out of the shoe.

"Oh, God." Mud oozed from between her toes. "Tell me this isn't happening."

Spencer could see she was beginning to lose her balance. "I've got you," he said, keeping hold of her hand and putting an arm around her waist. "If you can just move a few inches to your right—"

The folder slipped out of her hand. She tried to make a grab for it, and he tightened his arm around her just in time to save her from a face-plant. But then she unexpectedly scrambled for the paperwork again, and all control was lost.

In the next second she was sitting in the mud and gravel, muttering curses under her breath and glaring at him as if everything was his fault.

2

"WHAT HAPPENED TO 'I've got you'?" Erin asked, then realized her snappy tone wouldn't get her anywhere. Neither would glaring. She glanced down at the folder that she'd luckily salvaged, and pulled herself together before she looked up with as much concern as she could muster. "I hope I didn't get you dirty."

Spencer extended his hand, a wry expression on his face. "You can clean up inside," he said, sounding as though he'd rather have his arm broken than invite her into his home.

Dusty skidded to a stop inches short of the puddle. "Are you okay, Erin?" he asked as he bent to pull her shoe out of the mud.

It looked like she felt, but after a quick swipe over the bottom of her foot, she was able to slip it back on.

"Just mortified. I'll get over it." Again, she accepted Spencer's hand, and as he helped her to her feet, she realized her skirt had ridden up. She jerked her hand free to tug down the hem and fell flush against his hard chest.

She froze, making sure her feet were solidly planted before she made any more sudden moves. His arm immediately came around her. Her second mistake was to look up into his eyes. Spencer's expression remained detached, but something had turned his eyes a dark green.

"Sorry," she muttered. "And thanks." She lowered the hand she couldn't recall pressing to his chest and tentatively straightened. "I think it's safe to let me go."

He hesitated before releasing her. "Dusty, you mind moving Erin's car?"

"Sure thing. Are the keys in the ignition?"

Neither of them looked at Dusty. They were still gazing at each other. But it took her a few seconds to realize it.

She cleared her throat and watched the ground as she moved away from Spencer and turned to smile at the young man. "I'm already muddy. I might as well do it."

"It's no trouble. Anyway, you don't want to get your seats mucked up."

Spencer picked up a piece of paper that had fallen from her folder. When he straightened and handed it to her, she saw what she'd done to his flannel shirt. The dark blue-and-gray plaid couldn't hide the streaks of mud her fingers had left behind.

Erin cringed. "Sorry," she said, waving at his chest. "Of course I'll pay to have it cleaned."

His mouth twitched at the corner. It wasn't a smile exactly, but the closest thing to one that she'd seen on his face yet. "I have a washing machine and dryer if you want to use them before your next appointment."

"What?" She glanced down at herself and then over her shoulder to check the back. Of course she didn't have an appointment. She'd just said that as an excuse. "Dammit, this is a new skirt." And it belonged to Lila.

"It's only mud," Spencer said, eyeing the front of her legs. "It'll wash out."

"I hope so."

His gaze shifted briefly to Dusty, then back to Erin. “Are you coming?” Impatience flared in his face and extended to his voice. “I haven’t got all day.”

“Yes, thanks.”

Dusty hadn’t moved. He was staring at his boss with a puzzled frown. But one warning look from Spencer and Dusty opened the car door and hopped in.

Spencer didn’t even wait for her or offer his arm. Though the ground wasn’t muddy where they walked around to the back of the two-story brick house. Erin was five-five and he had to be over six feet, so it was hard keeping up with his much longer strides.

It felt good to get her circulation going, though. The autumn day had started off mildly enough, but the puddle had been cold, and the brisk wind sweeping off the foothills made her teeth chatter.

He held the door open and gestured her inside. She stopped on the thick woven floor mat and tried to scrape off her muddy right shoe, wishing she’d worn her usual Nikes. The heel caught in the roping. A discreet jerk didn’t help. Stooping or bending over wasn’t going to be fun. Or easy.

“Hold on a minute.” Spencer crouched behind her and lifted her foot out of the shoe, then freed the heel. “You want to leave these off for now?”

“Yes,” she said, feeling like a five-year-old, bracing her hands against the door frame and still clutching the folder. It not only held the contract but Lila’s list. “Thank you.”

Unexpectedly, he wrapped his fingers around her other ankle, and a jolt of heat shot up her leg. For a big guy with big hands, he had a gentle touch. She almost didn’t notice when his palm slid partway up her calf as he removed her other shoe.

"Don't worry about the floor," he said, and she realized he was waiting for her to move forward. "It's just the mudroom."

"Oh." She glanced at the parkas and jackets hanging on hooks, at the cubbyholes filled with heavy gloves. "I've never seen a mudroom before."

"On second thought, you'd better use this." Rising, he grabbed a towel hanging on the side of a deep utility sink. "I don't care about the floor, but you could slip."

He threw the towel on the tiles in front of her, his hand poised near her elbow, ready to catch her if she stumbled. His brown hair was a bit longer than last time but still pretty short. It was an expensive cut, not something a regular barber would do.

"Don't you have a rag? I don't want to stain your towel."

"That is a rag. Go ahead."

Probably a good thing he never smiled. Who knew what that would do to her? Normally, she wasn't a clumsy person. "I'm sure some of the homes in California have mudrooms, but not in the area where I grew up," she said, wiping the bottom of her feet on the rag. "Most people think of LA or Hollywood, but there are lots of ranches in the southern part of the state."

He looked as though he couldn't be less interested in her rambling. "Right through that door is the laundry room."

The nervous chatter wasn't like her. Not even around good-looking guys. And then it hit her. "I can't wash my clothes." She turned to look at him. "I have nothing to wear in the meantime."

Spencer ran his gaze down her body. "I'll find something for you."

"Oh, no, that's—" Erin stopped herself from rejecting

his offer. Why give up the extra time to convince him to sign the contract? She let out a breath. "That would be great."

He placed her heels in the sink, managing to look amused without even a hint of a smile, and gestured for her to keep moving.

Sunlight flooded in through a window in the laundry room. The washer and dryer both looked new and high-end. Above them was a row of dark wood custom cabinets. The room was narrow but well organized, with lots of shelves and hooks and hangers on the opposite wall.

"Come with me," he said, walking past her. "You can change in the bathroom while I get something for you to wear."

They walked into a large airy kitchen with gleaming wood floors and stainless steel appliances. The butcher-block island in the middle was the only thing that looked old.

"Is the house new?" she asked, skimming a hand over the smooth countertop. It wasn't granite but something similar.

"No, but I had some work done. There's the bathroom." He nodded at a door to their left and then headed for the staircase.

She hoped he'd give her a tour later. The place looked so much more interesting than it had from the outside. The open floor plan couldn't be part of the original layout, nor the oversize windows across the back that allowed a stunning view of the Rockies. Tastefully decorated in earth tones, it was nothing like the man cave she might've envisioned had she stopped to think about it.

There was some Western artwork on one wall and three framed pictures sitting on the mantel that she was dying to get a look at. But that could wait. She didn't want him to catch her snooping.

Just after she'd stripped off the skirt and was deciding on her top, which had only a few smudges, she heard the knock at the door. She opened it a little and peeked out. He held up a robe. Not one that belonged to him. It was light pink and on the small side.

"Your wife's?' she asked, startled at the thought.

"It's my mom's. She forgot it when she visited. She won't mind."

Well, hell… That didn't tell her anything. "Are you married?"

"No."

"Good." Erin almost choked on the word. She stared at Spencer, praying there was a chance she hadn't actually said it out loud.

His brows had risen slightly. "You want the robe or not?"

She grabbed it and shut the door.

Well, at least he wasn't laughing. Anyway, *good* could mean lots of things.

She finished undressing while keeping her eyes on the folder. All she needed to worry about was getting him to give his permission to film on his land. It was easy money, for heaven's sake. The crew would leave his property just as they found it, if not in even better condition.

By the time she'd slipped into the robe and made necessary adjustments so her bra wouldn't show, she could smell coffee. Spencer clearly liked his brew strong.

He was standing at the kitchen sink with his back to her, and she took advantage of the moment to study his long denim-clad legs and narrow hips. Great butt, good enough to be a body double…although she'd have to see him naked to know for sure.

He turned suddenly, as if he'd sensed her watching him. His gaze took in the robe, the exposed lower half of her calves and bare feet, before motioning with his chin. "You know where the laundry room is."

"Yep. Thanks."

Erin had been to so many Laundromats in her twenty-eight years that she thought she'd used every model and brand of washing machine on the market.

She was so wrong.

Studying the list of different cycles was getting her more excited than was probably healthy. But she didn't care, because this baby could do everything but make a bed. And she hadn't even looked at the dryer yet.

"Is there a problem?"

At the sound of Spencer's voice, she glanced at him standing in the doorway, but only briefly before she turned back to the washer. "Check this out…it has seven wash cycles and—"

"I'm aware."

"Oh, right." She'd already put in detergent and her clothes, set it for an extra-small load and cold water, then chose a cycle before moving over to the dryer. "As soon as I start making some real money, I'm getting a pair of these. You remember how much they cost?"

"Around thirty-five hundred, I think."

"Dollars?" She realized what she'd said the same second he tightened his mouth. Wow, he'd almost smiled again. "Go ahead and laugh." She turned to stroke the dryer. "I'd never have to iron again." Erin hadn't touched an iron in years. "Or wear wrinkled clothes."

"If you want, there's fabric softener and dryer sheets in the cabinet in front of you."

She'd seen them on the shelf above the laundry detergent. Everything was so clean and orderly, it kind of made her nervous. It wasn't that she was a slob or anything, but as soon as she'd started living out of a suitcase most of the time, her main priority was remembering to pack everything.

She opened the cabinet and knew reaching the second shelf was iffy. Even with raising herself on tiptoes, her fingertips only grazed the box of dryer sheets.

Spencer came up behind her and brought down the box. "How about the fabric softener?"

"No, thanks," she murmured, feeling his heat against her back. He wasn't actually touching her, but he wasn't giving her any space, either. Experimentally, she inched back, and it was like she'd hit a brick wall. Despite his lean build, he was solid muscle.

"Anything else?"

"Yeah," she said, turning around to face him. Her right breast grazed his arm, and a shiver raced down her spine. Spencer backed up a step. It didn't help. Hell, he'd have to leave the state before the flutters in her chest would stop. "How about we talk a little business while I'm waiting for my clothes?"

She'd always had a husky voice, even as a kid. But it sounded different, lower than usual, as though she might be coming down with a cold. Ignoring it, she waited for him to say something, not sure how long she'd be able to hold his piercing gaze.

The silence between them seemed to suspend time, which Erin didn't foolishly mistake for the possibility he'd changed his mind. A sudden chill coming from him took care of the fluttering problem.

"Okay, wait," she said, catching his arm when he turned to leave. "How about a tour of the house? Not the bedrooms or anything. Just, you know, common areas."

He stopped to stare pointedly at her hand. "Why? So you can see if all the cameras would fit?"

Erin sighed, hating the shift in his demeanor. "Come on, you can't blame me for trying…" she said, lowering her hand. "I know we got off to a rocky start. Completely my fault. I rushed in without explaining how it works. We're only asking for a two-week window to access your property. None of the crew would come anywhere near you or the house—"

"I don't blame you at all," he said, folding his arms across his chest. "In fact, if you have some other trick up your sleeve, go for it. Let's see what you got."

"Trick?" None of this made sense. He'd known all along why she was here. "You think I fell in the mud on purpose?"

"I don't know. Did you?"

"Of course not." She couldn't read him. Was he teasing, or trying to distract her? "I swear to you, the land would be left in perfect condition. And the money is more than generous." Pausing for a breath, she moistened her dry lips. "Better than the boilerplate." She wasn't lying. She'd nearly gotten her head chewed off for the offer she'd extended him.

His brows rose expectantly. "That's it?"

She stared at him, thoroughly confused.

"I have to admit, I'm disappointed," he said. "I expected something interesting. Not that it would've mattered. I'm not going to change my mind."

"Wait. Don't you have any questions for me? Whatever is holding you back might not be an issue at all. At least let me try to put your concerns to rest." She grabbed the folder off the dryer and followed him into the kitchen. "Can we do that?"

"Do what?"

"Start a discussion."

He poured coffee into a black mug and ignored the blue one that she presumed he'd set out for her. Leaning against the counter, he took a sip while staring at her over the rim. It wasn't so much his silence as the sudden narrowing of his eyes that unnerved her.

"What?"

"I do have a question."

"Great," she said, relaxing and pouring some coffee. Maybe they could come to terms after all. "Ask me anything."

"What exactly are you prepared to do to get me to agree?"

The sugar she was lightly sprinkling into her mug slipped for a moment. It wasn't so much his words but his tone that set off alarm bells. "I don't think I understand the question."

He gave her a slow smile. "I think you do."

She really hoped he wasn't implying what she thought… She looked up and followed his gaze to where the robe had slipped off her shoulder. The thick chenille fabric had taken her bra strap with it. Easy to assume she was naked underneath. So what? It didn't make his remark any less insulting.

Yanking the robe back in place, she returned his smile with a much sweeter one. "I'm willing to give you the benefit of the doubt and not assume you're being a complete prick."

SPENCER COULD SEE she was pissed. Maybe he'd gone too far. But after finding her *checklist*, he really hadn't known what to think at first. She was from Hollywood. The whole thing this afternoon could've been staged. Despite her claim she had no interest in acting, she'd transformed herself since they last met in July. The short skirt, the hair, the makeup…all of it meant to persuade him to give in. Yet the more they'd interacted, the less inclined he was to think she was playing him.

Either way, Erin was an interesting woman. Maybe he was fooling himself, but he didn't think he'd let on that he was attracted to her. Although he had a feeling celibacy had made him a poor judge. Even Dusty had given him a few strange looks.

"You're right. I was being a prick," he said, sorry she'd pulled the robe up. "That was an offensive insinuation, and I apologize."

"Oh." She studied him for several seconds, a slight frown tugging at her brows. "Apology accepted. So—"

"My land is still off-limits."

She let out a breath of pure frustration. "Will you at least tell me why?"

"Why do you want it so badly? There are thousands of acres of open land around here to choose from."

"It's about Moonlight Mountain. Jason, the director, wants to use the west side of the mountain in the last scene." Erin sighed. "I tried talking him out of it, but I admit I probably wasn't very convincing. If I were directing, I'd want to shoot the final showdown there myself. The setting is perfect."

"In your world I'm thinking the director is *god*."

"Pretty much." She shrugged. "This project is different, though. It's an indie film. No big money backers. Just a bunch of us who met in film school. We pooled our resources and connections to make this happen, so we're all invested in the film's success. We're hoping for a sequel. Without having to beg for backers. And best of all, at least for me," she said, grinning, "I get to be assistant *god*."

Spencer sipped his coffee to distract himself from the sparkle that turned her eyes a soft warm brown. He and Dusty had a lot of work to do before winter. So much that Spencer had actually considered hiring a couple men to help with fencing. He only had a small herd, but he didn't want to still be out repairing fences when the snow and frigid temperatures hit, let alone have to search for any wayward cattle that might escape in the meantime.

In the end he'd decided his privacy was more important. So he'd put off expanding operations; it wasn't easy, but he and Dusty had been tackling what needed doing from a prioritized list.

"Sorry to tell you," he said. "You played the sympathy card for nothing."

The warmth instantly disappeared, and she gave him a cool look. "I don't need your sympathy. You asked and I answered. Which is more courtesy than you extended me."

Hell, he didn't owe her a damn thing.

"Anyway, with or without your mountain, we will succeed. This is going to be the best damn film on a shoestring budget that was ever made. One way or another, Hollywood is going to stand up and take notice. Failure isn't an option. Not for me."

Not much he could say to that. He'd been that young and naive once. Erin hadn't learned enough about life yet. It had a way of sneaking up and knocking you down. He rubbed the scar on his wrist. It was a year old and already barely noticeable. He couldn't have found a better surgeon.

If only she could have mended his career, as well. His whole future had gone straight to hell that day. No more hopes and dreams for him.

"Good luck with that," he said, trying not to sound as cynical as he felt. "And by the way—" he dug into his jeans pocket and held out the piece of smudged paper with her list "—you dropped this."

3

ERIN STEPPED OUT of the Food Mart into the brisk morning air and shivered from head to toe. Her medium-weight black hoodie just wasn't cutting it anymore. It was perfect for fall, even winter, in Southern California. But not here in Blackfoot Falls.

But damned if she'd spend money on a coat. And damn Spencer Hunt's stubborn hide. She wouldn't even be here if it weren't for him.

Hugging a bag of groceries to her chest, she picked up the pace across the parking lot, nodding at an older man getting out of his truck, and wishing she'd driven from the inn. Fat lot of good the exercise would do her if she ended up a Popsicle.

Just before she reached the sidewalk, the sign for the new bakery caught her eye. If she was still here tomorrow, she'd check it out. Hell, she'd probably be stuck here for another week after screwing up so badly yesterday. For now, she stayed on the right side of the street with the sun shining directly on her.

Her cell rang, and hoping it was Lila, Erin pulled her hand out from the warmth of her jeans pocket. They'd been playing phone tag since yesterday's fiasco with Spencer.

"Finally," Erin said. "Where the hell have you been?"

"Don't you dare give me attitude." Lila was normally laid-back, but she sounded grumpy. "I'm so sick of *your friend* Jason and the damn princess…one minute she wants hair extensions, the next she's in my face over—Hey, did you know he's banging her?"

"Penelope? You sure?"

"Well, they were buttoning up when they left his trailer last night. So, you tell me."

Erin groaned. He wouldn't be the first director to sleep with his leading lady, but dammit… "Jason is too smart for that bullshit."

"I thought so, too, but I guess he just couldn't resist Ms. Lane's many charms. That woman is so impressed with herself it makes me gag."

"I hope you're not worried about your role in the sequel."

Lila hesitated. "A little bit," she admitted. "Penelope doesn't like me."

"Well, that's because you're so much prettier than she is." Erin ignored her friend's familiar sigh. Bias aside, it was the absolute truth. She also knew for a fact that Jason had been hot for Lila since college. "And even if they are screwing, it won't last," Erin said and then lowered her voice when a woman emerging from Abe's Variety store frowned at her. "They'll have moved on by the end of shooting. Anyway, Penelope is just a hired hand. We have equity in this project."

"Not much."

True. But Erin wasn't worried. "By the way, your list and accompanying tools of the trade sucked."

"My instructions were very detailed. What happened?"

"I hope I can get the mud out of your heels and denim skirt."

"Mud? Ah, jeez, Erin. What did you do?"

"I fell on my ass, that's what. And that wasn't even the worst part. He found the list you gave me."

After a startled squeak, Lila asked, "Why on earth did you have it with you?"

"Why do you think? To remind myself to smile and be charming."

Lila burst out laughing. "You're lying."

"Like hell. He asked if I'd be willing to sleep with him to get the contract signed."

"Well, you did say he was pretty hot."

Erin stopped in the middle of the sidewalk. "I can't believe you just said that."

"Because I know he didn't come out and ask any such thing. You wouldn't be so calm about it."

"Ah." Erin shivered and started moving again. "Okay, so I paraphrased, but the implication was there."

"And you said?"

"I might've *implied* he was a prick."

Lila sighed. "Do me a favor? Don't tell Jason yet."

"Tell him what? I'm not giving up. Hunt left the house before I could take another run at him. I'm going back out there later."

"Wait. You were in his house?"

"Yep, waiting while your clothes were in the wash." Hearing her friend's soft whimper, Erin winced. God, they both knew better. Erin in heels? That was just begging for an accident. "Anyway, he didn't give me time to explain about the list before he took off on horseback." Although she doubted an explanation existed that wouldn't end up making her sound hopeless. "I couldn't even snoop around. Dusty, the kid who works for him, was there. He told me Spencer rarely leaves the ranch."

The words were barely out of her mouth when a late-model silver truck passed her. For a second she thought she saw Spencer at the wheel.

"Ooh," Lila said. "That's why he's so mysterious. People around town don't know anything about him. I can't wait to see for myself—"

A block down, the truck pulled to the curb. A man climbed out and set a tan cowboy hat on his head.

"Hey," Erin said, cutting Lila short. "I gotta go. I think his royal hotness just made an appearance."

She disconnected, not trusting herself to walk and talk at the same time. She couldn't see his face, but the tall, lean body was right. So was the short dark hair. And she vaguely recalled seeing a silver truck parked near the barn yesterday.

He glanced around before closing the car door. That is, he looked just about everywhere except in her direction. So, yep, that was Spencer, and she'd bet Lila's designer stilettos that he'd spotted her, too. He could've kept going, but he hadn't, so that was promising.

Glad for her old comfy Nikes, she sped up as she watched him round the hood and then drop an envelope in the mailbox near the diner. She half expected him to go inside, but he was already retracing his steps back to the driver's side.

"Spencer, wait," she yelled, switching to a jog.

He paused briefly, at least long enough for her to know he'd heard, and then he opened the door.

The hell with that.

She stuck two fingers in her mouth and whistled loud enough to wake the dead. And because he'd ignored her to begin with, she added, "Yo, Spencer."

Everyone who was out and about on Main Street turned to look.

First, they glanced at her.

And then people stared at him.

Apparently he was more interesting. Probably due to his reputation for being a hermit. She'd bet half the town knew who she was from her last visit.

A small, wiry woman wearing an oversize World's Best Grandma sweatshirt stopped pushing a stroller to give him a once-over. Two old-timers leaving the diner eyeballed him as they dug out their chewing tobacco.

Unsmiling, Spencer nodded at the men.

Erin couldn't see what he'd done to get the World's Best Grandma moving. But she seemed anxious to be on her way. So did a young blonde walking her little white poodle.

"I'm surprised to see you in town," Erin said and leaned against his ridiculously clean truck. "Did you miss me?"

Spencer bit off a startled laugh and shook his head. "Haven't you left yet?"

"Um…" She glanced down at her beat-up Nikes and well-worn jeans. "Nope. Still here," she said and straightened when he pulled his door open wider. "Come into the diner with me. I'll buy you coffee. Or breakfast. Have you eaten yet? Marge makes great cinnamon rolls. And chocolate chip pancakes."

"No, thanks." He took off his hat and slid in behind the wheel.

"Wait." She shot forward, laying a hand on his arm, stopping him from pulling the handle. "Spencer, please," she said, finding herself sandwiched between him and the door. Not one of her better ideas. He smelled too damn good. His slightly parted lips were too tempting. The awareness darkening his eyes made it difficult for her to breathe. She was standing too close, but she couldn't make herself move away.

"Please what?" he asked softly, then waited for an answer she couldn't seem to articulate. "I can't give you what you want, Erin."

She wanted him to touch her.

The thought came from nowhere and wrenched her out of fantasyland.

"Look," she said, inching back, "I'm sorry I whistled and called attention to you. That wasn't cool. But I'd really like to explain about the list you found yesterday."

An air horn honked ungodly loud and close.

Grimacing, she covered her ear.

Spencer pulled her against him just as a truck sped by. The door closed behind her, biting into her back while her breasts pressed against his arm. It was unnecessary. The truck hadn't passed close enough to hit her, but she wasn't complaining.

When the teenage boys riding in the truck's bed laughed and jeered, she realized then the driver had purposely swerved just to scare them. If Erin had been anywhere else, she would've flipped them off. Or maybe not, since her heart was pounding so hard the roar had reached her ears. Even her legs were shaky. Damn kids.

"Are you all right?" Spencer's arm had tightened around her, and he was trying to look at her face.

"I don't think they got your door." She would've heard the metals scraping together. "Did they?" She turned to see for herself, but Spencer caught her chin and forced her to meet his eyes.

"Forget about the truck. I yanked the door pretty hard trying to get you out of the way."

"I'm fine." She lowered her gaze and focused on the

muscle working in his jaw. "Stupid kids." Her heart was still racing, and her knees had lost their starch, but that had more to do with the feel of his warm breath on her cheek.

"You'll bruise."

"Maybe it'll match yesterday's…" She shrugged, noticed her palm pressed to his chest and blinked. When had that happened?

Resisting the urge to snatch her hand back, she casually reached up and brushed a loose strand of hair away from her face.

Spencer glanced down Main Street and lowered his arm. "It's clear. Come on, hop in. I'll give you a ride."

She didn't give him a chance to change his mind. After a quick peek for herself, she hurried around and jumped into the passenger seat.

"Where are you headed?" he asked as he pulled out.

"I don't know. Where are you going?"

His mouth lifted in a slight smile. "I can drop you off on the next block if you want."

A sudden flash of memory had her peering into her bag. "Damn." Both Twinkies were flat. No problem, she'd eat them, anyway. Of course the carton of dip had survived, because the bag of corn chips was now crumbs.

"Groceries?"

"Yep. Oh, well." She offered him a candy bar. "It's only smashed on the end."

"No, thanks."

She rooted around and found another. "How about this one? It doesn't look too bad."

He took his eyes off the road to frown at her just as they passed the inn where she was staying. Next was a gas station, and after that, nothing but open highway and a scattering of large ranches.

Spencer lowered his gaze to the bag. "Is there anything healthy in there?"

Fishing out the dip, she pretended to study the ingredient list. "It's green, so probably," she said and hid a smile at his look of revulsion. "The chips got smashed, though. But I bet we can make it work."

"Are you serious?"

"I'm starving. This is breakfast. Oh, I should've asked…do you care if I eat in your truck?"

He shook his head, his expression puzzled. "It's all junk food."

"Look, I'd love to be dining on delicious organic salads and fruit every day. But even if the Food Mart did carry organic produce, it's not in my budget."

"You must have an expense account and per diem."

"Sort of." She unwrapped a Twinkie and broke it in half. "Motel rooms are covered, within reason, of course, and I'm reimbursed for gas. I'm using my own car, and I pay for my food." She bit into her half and offered him the other.

It came as no surprise when he turned down the Twinkie with a single lifted brow.

"I have a bag of organic apples that I brought with me. It's in my room." Feeling a bit defensive, she stuffed the rest of the cake into her mouth. She hated that she hadn't completely kicked her college junk food habit. But what she'd told him was true. She had to watch her pennies.

"And that room would be where?"

Shit.

She looked at him, pointed to her mouth and kept

chewing, wondering how long she could stall. God, she'd kill for some coffee.

The scenery was beautiful. Her gaze skipped the scrubby brush closer to the road and took in the mix of pines, cottonwoods and quaking aspen covering the foothills of the Rockies. Fall had come late to this corner of the country. Some of the lower altitude trees still had orange-and-gold leaves clinging to the branches.

Not that she held any hope the landscape would distract Spencer. She fully expected him to make a U-turn at any second.

Deciding not to push his patience, she swallowed the last of the Twinkie and said, "I'm staying at The Boarding House Inn."

"The same Boarding House Inn we passed five minutes ago?"

"Yep. The place is pretty cool. It really was a boardinghouse at one time." Waiting for him to lay into her, she studied his hand resting on the steering wheel. His long, lean fingers looked elegant and graceful, with trimmed fingernails that seemed too neat and clean to belong to a cowboy. "Do you play the piano?"

The truck veered to the shoulder. He'd put both hands on the wheel as he prepared to make a turn. They hit a rock, and the sudden jerk had her reaching for the dashboard.

"Wait. Please, don't," she said just as a second bump jarred her poor bruised butt and made her wince. "Can I come with you?"

Spencer stopped the truck and sent her a curious look. "You don't even know where I'm going."

"It doesn't matter. It's warm in here, and I don't have anything better to do."

“So, why are you hanging around town, wasting money on lodging?”

“Well, if you’re going to resort to logic, forget it. I have nothing to say.”

He sighed and shifted to Neutral. “I’m not changing my mind.”

“I know.” And she wasn’t giving up the fight. “Actually, I do have a few things to take care of, like getting some pictures of the new storefronts in town. It’s crazy how much has changed in three months.”

“That shouldn’t take long.”

She stared at him. “You really do want to get rid of me. Okay.” She didn’t know what else to say. She’d always been outgoing and people generally liked her. “I’d offer to walk back if it weren’t so freezing, so if you wouldn’t mind…”

Shaking his head and looking resigned, he shifted to Drive. “I’m going to the Lone Wolf, a ranch about twelve miles from here.” He glanced at her. “If you want to come along.”

She nodded enthusiastically.

Spencer kept his foot on the brake and his attention on her. “On one condition.”

Erin stopped herself from rolling her eyes. “I don’t nag you about using your land.”

“Good girl.” He almost smiled. “You’re catching on.”

Good girl.

Gritting her teeth, she tore off a piece of Twinkie from the remaining half and stuffed it in her mouth before she ended up saying something snarky. God, did she hate not having the upper hand. She had to be nice no matter what, and Spencer knew it. He also knew she hadn't folded. But she'd stick to the deal and not pester him for the rest of the day.

"Now, you want to tell me about that list of yours?"

4

SHE WAS TROUBLE. That was undeniable. And Spencer had gone out of his way looking for it. Something about the damn woman stirred a primal craving in him that he'd thought had died along with his career.

Part of the attraction was her husky voice. The low sexy timbre rasped against his skin and hijacked his brain. It made him wonder what her fingernails would feel like raking his back. Made it too easy for a man to get lost. Maybe even agree to something he'd later regret.

Carefully keeping his eyes on the road, he listened to her explanation about her friend's involvement with the crazy list. But he hadn't caught much of it. Only that it made sense someone else had put her up to changing her appearance. Three months ago, when she'd first turned up at Shadow Creek, she'd worn jeans and a T-shirt, her long hair clipped up and kind of messy.

Yesterday she'd looked ready for a date.

He sensed movement and glanced over at her. She'd loosened the neck of the black sweatshirt and let the hood fall to her back. Sunlight picked up caramel-colored strands of the brown hair he'd formerly considered unremarkable. Her eyes were nearly the same golden caramel shade. She had a small pert nose and a wide mouth. Her habit of pursing those full lips while she was thinking would definitely torment him if he let it.

"…Lila can pull off that sort of stuff. I'm hopeless. Oh, and thanks again for letting me use the washer and dryer. It was Lila's skirt. And heels." She paused to pull a can of Red Bull out of her bag and offered it to him. He shook his head. "Not my favorite, but I've had only two cups of coffee today."

He shot her a questioning look.

"I'm a total caffeine junkie," she explained. "It started in college."

"Too many all-night parties?"

"I wish. More like late-night studying. And working part-time."

"Where did you go?"

"UCLA. They have a great film school." She popped the can. "Did you go to college?"

"Yep. No place you'd recognize."

"Ah."

Hell, he had to be more careful. Not ask questions that could be turned back on him. He'd kept to himself for so long he was out of practice. And with someone like Erin…the woman was an open book, frank and matter-of-fact. Maybe that was how she got people to feel comfortable. Convince them to open their homes and lives to her. Something he'd better keep in mind. And not recklessly invite her on ride-alongs.

"So, why are we going to the Lone Wolf?" she asked.

"I have some business with the owner, Matt Gunderson. I can't speak for why you're tagging along."

Erin grinned. "It's pretty out here. So different from when I was here in July."

After putting the bag on the floorboard, she tucked her free hand under her thigh. Hunching her shoulders, she looked cold. He was still wearing the fleece-lined jacket he'd put on to feed the horses before he left, so he hadn't bothered with the heater.

He turned it on. "Feel free to adjust the temperature."

She was right on it. "Tell me if it gets too warm for you."

"I have a question."

"Okay." She wedged the can between her legs and rubbed her palms together in front of the vent as she looked at him.

A slew of lusty thoughts raced through Spencer's mind. All because of where she'd innocently stuck the damn can, he thought with disgust. Although, in his defense, it didn't help that he'd seen her bare thighs. Nice and toned, they'd feel real good gripping his waist.

Images of her in that short denim skirt had haunted him late into the night. No surprise he'd woken up harder than a rock.

It wasn't her. It was him. He hadn't gone without sex this long since the summer between sophomore and junior years of high school. Hell, he was probably going through withdrawal.

"So, let me get this straight—your friend Lila gave you the makeover advice. Obviously to get my attention..." He saw Erin fidget, and he purposely drew out the suspense as he navigated a curve in the road. "And then what? You were willing to sleep with me to get—"

"No." She barked the word, then folded her arms across her chest. "I mean, I would—but not to get you to—" She huffed with aggravation. "The short answer is *no*."

"We have another five minutes to the Lone Wolf. Plenty of time for the long answer."

He'd meant to tease her, but it backfired. The pink in her cheeks and the fire in her eyes were making him hot and prickly. Maybe he was reading into it, but it was possible they shared the same itch. He had to really think about how he wanted this to play out.

"To soften you up, I guess," she said, though he hadn't expected an answer. "It's kind of funny. There's no way in hell I'd have sex with you in exchange for Moonlight Mountain—"

Spencer snorted a laugh. "You'd have to be damn good to expect me to give you the whole mountain."

"You know what I mean," she said, leveling a cool gaze his way. "And had you let me finish, I was about to say that under any other circumstance, yeah, damn right I would've slept with you."

He almost missed the turn. Spotting the road marker at the last second, he wrenched the steering wheel. Erin threw out both arms and flattened her palms against the dashboard. His Stetson tumbled off the console onto the floor.

"Sorry," he mumbled.

"I guess that was partly my fault."

Deep ruts in the gravel road worked against him as he righted the truck. The ground was still muddy, some patches slick from the wet fall leaves. All he needed was to get stuck out here; with Erin, no less.

Erin and the self-satisfied smirk she was trying to hide.

Spencer knew some bold women back in Boise, and Erin, being strong and plainspoken, shouldn't have surprised him. But he had to admit, he hadn't seen that coming.

The moment they were back on track, all tires accounted for, he said, "So you're saying if we'd met at the bar in town and had no business connection, you would've gone home with me."

"I don't know." She narrowed her eyes at him. "Maybe. But I wouldn't have gone to your place."

"The inn?"

"You know what? It's a moot point." She shifted in her seat, adjusted the air vents again. "Let's drop it."

"You opened the door."

"Yeah, well, now I'm closing it."

Spencer smiled to himself. He'd finally figured out her strategy. She thought dangling sex and knocking him off balance would give her the upper hand. And damn, she wasn't completely wrong. "Humor me. I'm curious."

She huffed out a disgruntled sigh. "Look, I don't pick up guys in bars, okay? And if I did, I sure as hell wouldn't let them know where I live. Or go to some strange man's place. That would be pretty stupid."

"So, what? You'd prefer to have sex in a car? A hotel?"

"What part of moot point don't you understand?" Staring at him, she shook her head. "Like I said, circumstances being what they are, it doesn't matter."

"Well, I'm never going to let you and your people set foot on the mountain."

"And I'll never quit trying to wear you down. Today you get a pass. I intend to honor the condition of my ride-along. But after that..." She shrugged, her lips curving in a cocky smile.

Spencer couldn't believe he was having this conversation. Or worse, that he wouldn't let it go. "I'm flat out telling you Moonlight Mountain is off-limits," he said and caught her smile slip a bit. "So there's no reason for sex to be off the table."

"Since I'm confident I can change your mind, sex definitely can't be part of the equation. It would feel too creepy." She straightened in her seat and peered up ahead at the buildings starting to become visible. "Is that the Lone Wolf?"

"I think so. I've only been out here once before."

"Looks big."

"Yep." He tried not to sound like a sulky ten-year-old. Especially since Erin didn't seem to give a shit one way or the other about having sex. But in truth, he was used to getting his way. Up until the accident that had changed everything, his life had been golden.

HE PARKED THE TRUCK close to a structure that Erin guessed was the barn. The ranch in general was a sizable spread with a large stable, what looked to be a second barn, a dozen or more corrals and a building large enough to be a warehouse.

She opened the door and frowned at the soft ground around them. It was a big truck, and she was too high up to just hop out. Climbing in had been easy because she'd had a boost from the curb.

"Here." Spencer was suddenly standing there offering his hand. When she hesitated, he added, "I won't bite."

"No, but will you let me fall on my ass?"

"You don't need my help for that."

"Ha. Funny." Eyeing his boots, she saw they were making a slight depression in the dirt. She took his hand and not for the first time wondered why he didn't have more calluses.

She stepped down and was instantly glad for his assistance. He didn't let go until they reached a patch of gravel, and she was sure of her footing.

"I know her," Erin murmured when she finally looked up and caught sight of a woman standing on the porch of an attractive two-story house set back from everything. "I think that's Rachel." Her long, beautiful auburn hair wasn't easily forgotten. Still, Erin glanced at Spencer for confirmation.

He shrugged. "Could be Matt's wife. I've never met her." His attention shifted to the second barn. "Here's Gunderson now."

Spencer walked toward the man, until they met up and shook hands. They were around the same height, somewhere just over the six-foot mark, though Matt had a huskier build and lighter hair.

Erin trailed behind until Spencer introduced her. Matt's rough palm felt more like what she expected of a cowboy. She knew from the townspeople that Spencer was new to the area. And damn, she was curious about what he'd been doing before buying Shadow Creek Ranch. If she could get Dusty alone, she bet he would tell her.

"Ah, here comes Rachel," Matt said, looking toward the house.

"I thought it was her," Erin said and caught Matt's confused expression. "We met in town about three months ago. I was here scouting locations for a film."

"Okay. You must be with that independent film, then," Matt said, and she nodded. "My buddy Ben Wolf has been providing your production company with some stock."

"That's right. I don't know Ben all that well, but we

met when he was still working in Hollywood. He sure has some beautiful horses."

Matt nodded at Spencer. "How do you figure into all this?"

"I don't," he said, putting up both hands. "I just gave the lady a ride."

Erin grinned. "I'm trying to get him to let us use Moonlight Mountain. The director wants to shoot the last scene of the movie on the west ridge."

"I can see why. Nice piece of real estate you've got there," Matt said to Spencer. "I'd considered making an offer on it myself, but I think you'd already put down earnest money."

"Well, damn. I wish you had bought it. Spencer's playing hard to get."

"Don't start," he warned in a low voice just as Rachel approached.

"Oh, please, I haven't even begun to get started." Erin smiled sweetly, heard Matt chuckle, then turned to Rachel.

"Erin, right?"

"Yes, we met at— Oh—" Erin stumbled back a step. Rachel was a hugger. "Okay," Erin murmured, doing her best to reciprocate but feeling awkward. She kind of patted the other woman's back and hoped that was enough.

Matt grinned but not without a hint of understanding in his face. "You meet Rachel once, and you're a friend for life."

"Not everyone." Rachel glanced at her husband. "You know who I'm talking about," she said and turned to Spencer with a smile and her hand out. "Hello. I'm Rachel."

He shifted the speculative look he was giving Erin,

his expression easing as he nodded at Rachel. "Spencer Hunt." He reached up and yanked off his hat before shaking her hand. "Pleased to meet you, Rachel."

With raised brows, Rachel looked at her husband.

"Ah, Christ." Matt rubbed his jaw, the corners of his mouth twitching. "Thanks, Hunt. Yeah, thanks for showing up the rest of us poor slobs with your fancy manners."

"You can blame my mama for that." Spencer reset the hat on his head and smiled. A real, honest-to-goodness, genuine smile that seemed to come so naturally.

Wow. Erin hadn't known he had it in him. "You've never removed your hat for me," she said.

He turned to her with a hint of amusement in his face. "If you were less irritating, maybe I would."

Matt choked out a laugh. Then something caught his attention, and he excused himself, moving to the side. "Hey, Chuck," he called to a young man walking toward the corral. "Have you seen Petey?"

"I think he's in the bunkhouse."

"Mind getting him for me?"

"No problem, boss."

Rachel's lips were pressed together as she studied Spencer and then Erin. "Are you guys headed to the stable?"

Erin shrugged. "I don't even know why we're here."

Matt rejoined them. "Yep, we'll be in the stable for a while. Maybe take a ride out to the north pasture. We'll end up at the house eventually. Are you going to be home?"

Rachel nodded. "I put a roast in the slow cooker. It won't be ready until closer to dinnertime. But I can make some coffee for now, and sandwiches later."

Coffee? The magic word.

Erin resisted the urge to raise her hand and jump up and down.

"I'm sure there's coffee brewing in the stable or the barn. I'll call you in a while." Matt smiled and kissed Rachel. "Thanks, honey."

It was just a brief brushing of lips, but it was the tenderness in his eyes that made Erin's chest ache. No man had ever looked at her like that. And probably never would. In the thirty-three years her parents had been married, she'd never seen them kiss or hug each other even once. But then she hadn't seen much of them, period. They'd worked a lot, so she'd mostly hung out at Lila's house after school.

"Erin? You want to come to the house with me?" Rachel asked. "Or would you prefer to go with the guys and learn everything you didn't want to know about storing and shipping frozen bull semen?"

With a laugh, Erin looked at the men. Seeing their wry smiles, she realized it wasn't a joke. "Huh." She turned back to Rachel. "So, you mentioned coffee?"

"I can even make you an espresso if you want." Rachel checked her watch. "Damn. We have to hurry. The chocolate chip cookies are almost ready to come out of the oven."

"Seriously? You made cookies?" Erin said, in awe of her new hero.

"They're actually the slice-and-bake stuff," Rachel whispered as they started for the house. "But honestly, they taste homemade, so don't tell anyone."

Erin slowed and glanced back at Spencer. "Don't leave without me..."

He'd been watching her. Rather boldly for a reserved man who guarded his privacy. Made her wonder just how well he knew Matt. And what exactly he was trying to do, besides give her a coronary.

"Better save me a bite," Spencer said with a wink.

"Go worry about your semen."

She hadn't noticed the cowboy leaving the barn until he burst out laughing.

Grinning, Rachel was darting glances at Spencer when Erin fell into step beside her.

"Uh-uh." Erin shook her head. "I know that look. It's not like that."

"How do you know what I'm thinking?"

"Because you remind me of my friend Lila, and she would be looking at me just like you are right now."

Rachel's smile widened.

"I barely know him. Since the minute we met, he's been trying to get rid of me."

"I've seen him only once, and it was from a distance," Rachel said. "He's very good-looking."

"Yes, he is. And stubborn. Annoying as hell." Erin almost sneaked another look but caught herself. "I mean, who wouldn't jump at the chance to make a small bundle for doing nothing?"

"I take it you want to do some filming on his property?"

Erin nodded. "He owns a lot of land, but his ranch isn't that big. His herd is small. It's hard to believe he makes so much money that he could afford to—" Erin frowned. "Is frozen semen big business?"

"It can be," Rachel said. "If you have the right stock to begin with. Matt raises rodeo stock. So far he's bred two champion bulls and a winning stallion, and he hasn't been at it very long. He's just started to research the feasibility of selling the semen."

"How does Spencer fit into it?"

"Other than he knows about proper storage and shipping, I'm not really sure."

Erin didn't believe that for a second. Not with the way Rachel purposely avoided eye contact. Good to know she was trustworthy or simply not the type to gossip. Either way, she'd earned Erin's respect.

"Hey, do those chocolate chip cookies have nuts in them?" Erin asked as they reached the porch of the well-kept two-story house with green shutters.

"Of course." Rachel looked insulted. "If I'm going to cheat and pass them off as my own, why on earth would I skimp?"

Erin grinned. A woman after her own heart.

5

AFTER A TWO-HOUR tour of the Lone Wolf, Spencer decided he liked Gunderson. They'd met twice before, once by chance, the second time to size each other up. But today was the day of reckoning. Spencer could tell a lot about a man by the way he treated his animals, his hired men and his wife. Matt Gunderson excelled in all three areas, and if he wanted Spencer's help, he was inclined to do what he could.

"I wish I could give you more assurance. Frozen semen has an indefinite shelf life as long as it isn't thawed. On the downside you have to have the facility to properly store it," Spencer said, his arms propped on the door of King Arthur's stall. The handsome black stallion looked to be in perfect health. "I hear there's a big demand in the overseas market. Chilled semen is only fertile for one to three days after it's collected. Too many variables can eat up the time real quick before it gets to its destination."

Matt nodded. "On the other side of the coin, the semen doesn't always survive the freezing process. I read that roughly 25 percent of the stallion population freezes well. Would you agree with that?"

"I'm reading the same research you are," Spencer said, shrugging.

"Yeah, but I'm guessing you understand most of it better than I do."

Spencer smiled. Besides Dusty, Gunderson was the only person in Blackfoot Falls who knew anything about Spencer. So maybe Rachel did, as well. His thoughts skipped straight to Erin, who could be grilling Rachel right now, looking for a way to convince him to lease her Moonlight Mountain. Matt knew to be discreet, and Spencer hoped Rachel followed his lead.

And if not, nothing he could do about it at this point. It wasn't as though he harbored some horrible secret—he just didn't care to revisit that less than shining moment that cost him everything. And the pitying looks... yeah, he could do without those.

"Look," Spencer said, "you can probably expect another 50 percent to freeze acceptably. You have prime animals, and if you make sure you're offering only the highest quality semen, you'll have more customers than you can handle."

King Arthur neighed loudly and shook his mane.

Matt grinned. "This guy is something else. It'll break my heart if I can't keep some viable semen."

"He sired any foals yet?"

"Two. I sold one, and my friend Ben has the other. The next one I'm keeping."

"I wish I could've helped you out today." Spencer glanced at his watch. "I know you're more interested in bulls, but it's a different story trying to get them registered."

"I only want the semen for my own breeding purposes, so that's not a problem. Basically, I've got to figure out if I want to move forward and build a facility and find the right personnel to handle that portion of the business. Hell, I wasn't even interested in any of this until a few months ago."

Matt stepped away from the stall and headed for the pot of coffee he'd started. "You want some?" Matt asked.

"Sure." Spencer's thoughts wandered back to Erin. Time had flown by. He hadn't expected to be here this long, and he was a little surprised she hadn't come looking for him. Unless Rachel had given her a ride to town.

He didn't like that idea, even though he should. Sometimes she was a bit hard to read. Damn, he wished he knew if she was serious about sex being nonnegotiable. Maybe it was part of her strategy to get him to come around. The plan had merit. Not that he'd admit it.

"There's another way I'd consider getting into this business." Matt held out the mug of black coffee. "Go in with a partner—50/50 investment, 50/50 profit."

Spencer smiled. "I figured this discussion might be headed in that direction."

"You interested in that route?"

"It's possible." Spencer took a sip. "Are you looking to breed strictly rodeo stock?"

"For me, personally? Yeah, mostly." Matt gestured to King Arthur. "But when a stallion like this comes along, I'd be stupid not to consider other options. A guy I know, lives about twenty miles east of town...he trains racehorses. Trent's good. He's got several major wins under his belt. He's expressed some interest." Matt sipped from his mug, his expression thoughtful. "So, here's another question for you."

"Shoot."

"What's your opinion on cloning?"

Spencer almost spit out his coffee. "Are you serious?"

Matt laughed. "I'm just curious. Hell, I'd have to clone myself to take on any more work."

"You must be following all that Quarter Horse Association business down in Texas. That fight's been going on for a long time, and I don't see it ending soon."

"I agree with you there," Matt said, then they both turned when someone entered the stable.

It was Erin.

Her hair was mussed and her cheeks flushed. She'd taken off the hoodie and was down to a red T-shirt that fit snugly across her breasts and showed off toned, lightly tanned arms. Whether or not she was wearing a bra wasn't clear, but Spencer could see her nipples poking at the worn material.

"Speaking of trouble," he said when she was close enough to hear.

"Ah, you missed me. How sweet."

Matt chuckled just as his phone buzzed. "Excuse me a minute."

As they watched him walk away, Spencer noticed some hay in her hair. "Where were you?"

"Horseback riding. It was amazing."

"With Rachel?"

"No, she had to run over to the Sundance and drop something off, so Bobby took me." Erin hunched her shoulders and rubbed her arms. "It was warm out in the sun, but now I wish I'd put my hoodie back on."

Spencer shrugged out of his jacket.

"What are you doing?" She leaned away when he tried to drape it over her shoulders. "You'll be cold."

"I'm fine."

"Bobby said he has an extra jacket if I need it."

"Look, you're shivering. Can you just put the damn thing on without arguing?"

She pressed her lips together, her jaw clenched as he settled the heavy suede jacket around her. "Oh." She relaxed as he overlapped the front. "Wow. This is nice. Fleece-lined and everything. You might not get it back."

The jacket dwarfed her, hitting just above her knees. She turned her head and buried half her face into the collar, closing her eyes and inhaling deeply. A soft smile lifted her lips. She looked so damned sexy. Did she even realize what she was doing? She could be purposely taunting him, but he didn't think so.

Spencer cleared his throat. "Where did you go for your ride?"

She opened her eyes and blinked at him. "Into the foothills. Bobby said I did really well, considering it was only my second time on a horse."

"Uh-oh," Matt said as he joined them. "What did Bobby do now?"

Erin grinned. "He was very concerned about bringing me back in one piece. I heard about what happened with those women from the Sundance getting more than they bargained for."

Matt shook his head. "That kid is gonna be the death of me yet. He's a good worker and loves animals but doesn't have a lick of common sense."

"He shouldn't have taken you into the foothills," Spencer said, which earned him an indignant frown. "Too many steep and narrow trails for an inexperienced rider."

"We were careful, and as you can see, I'm perfectly fine."

"And damn lucky," Matt added. "Spencer's right. Especially with all the rain we've been having. A horse could lose his footing in the mud."

Erin sighed. "Please, don't say anything to Bobby. I practically begged him to take me."

Spencer didn't believe that and could tell Matt didn't, either. But Spencer had said enough, so he kept quiet.

"Which horse did he give you?" Matt asked.

"Caramel. She was very gentle."

"The small bay mare? At least she's a good choice for a beginning rider. She knows the trails."

"See?" Erin smiled. "Bobby did good. Anyway, Mr. Gunderson," she said with raised brows, "guys willing to climb on the backs of crazy bulls have no room to talk." She glanced at Spencer. "Did you know he's a world champion bull rider?" she added, then turned back to Matt. "I saw your gold buckles."

He shrugged. "Another lifetime," he said and nodded at Spencer. "You've done some rodeoing yourself."

Jesus. Why the hell did this have to come up now? Gunderson couldn't know much, but Spencer shouldn't be surprised that the man had looked him up. Matt was a smart guy. He wouldn't be putting out feelers for a partner unless he'd done some digging.

"Not professionally," Spencer said finally.

"I heard you were pretty damn good."

"Another lifetime." He met Matt's eyes, and a quiet understanding passed between them.

Erin was staring at him with enough curiosity to power the whole ranch.

"You ready?" he asked, before she could start with the questions. "I need to get going."

"Rachel invited us to stay for an early dinner. She should be back any second." Pulling the jacket tighter around her shoulders, Erin waited for his reply with wide hopeful eyes.

"You should stay," Matt said. "Rachel makes a mean pot roast."

"I heard my name." The woman herself walked into the stable. "Supper will be ready in thirty minutes. I know it's early, but since no one had lunch—"

Spencer shook his head. "Thanks, but not today."

"Okay, you get one rain check. That's it," Rachel said with a teasing smile, then looked at Erin. "If you'd like to stay, I can run you back to town later."

Erin's brief hesitation made Spencer tense. He'd be better off if she stayed. There'd be no nosy questions all the way back to town.

"It wouldn't be any trouble," Rachel added. "I even have a jacket that would fit you."

"That's really nice..." Erin's gaze drifted to Spencer.

He shrugged. "Whatever works for you, but I'm heading back now."

She slipped his jacket off her shoulders and held it out to him. So, she was staying. Why the hell was he disappointed?

"Hang on to it," he said. "The temperature is supposed to be dropping soon."

"Oh, you're not getting rid of me that easily. I'm just giving you your jacket back so you don't freeze," she said, then turned to Rachel. "Do I get a rain check, too?"

"Sure." Rachel smiled, her curious gaze sweeping over them. "What are you two doing tomorrow night?"

FIVE MINUTES AFTER they hit the road, Spencer broke the silence. "You're too quiet."

"Does that worry you?"

"A little bit."

Erin smiled. She was dying to ask him about his rodeo days, but she figured that might get her booted out of the truck. Anyway, she knew he was expecting to get hit with a barrage of questions. Which meant he had his guard up.

No problem. She could be patient.

Snuggling down into the jacket he'd refused to take, she adjusted the collar to cover her frozen ears and stuffed her hands deep into the warmth of the pockets. Even wearing the hoodie underneath she wasn't too warm at all. No getting around it, she would have to break down and spring for a pair of good cold-weather gloves.

"I wonder if Rachel made biscuits to go with the pot roast?" Erin murmured, still dreaming about the meal that could've been…

Spencer let out a laugh. "What did you say?"

"How could you turn down a home-cooked meal? I can't remember what anything but fast food tastes like."

"You could've stayed."

"I didn't want to put Rachel out." She shifted in the seat to get comfortable and heard a crackling pop. Glancing down, she lifted her heel off the forgotten bag of groceries. "Oh, great."

Spencer looked over at her and chuckled again.

"I just demolished the rest of my chips. How is that amusing?"

His gaze slid down to the jacket she'd turned into a cocoon. She could barely see over the collar. "What are you going to do when the weather really gets cold?"

"Stay indoors until it warms up."

"Good luck with that."

Erin sighed. From checking online, she knew the area was in for some bone-chilling winter temperatures, but she'd expected to be gone by then. "I need gloves."

With a dry look, he nodded at the glove compartment. "In there."

"No, that's not what I meant. I have to buy a pair. But I don't know what kind. I assume Abe carries a range at his store?"

"I wouldn't know."

"You've never been inside?"

"Nope."

"Why is that?"

Spencer abruptly turned his attention to the highway. Probably thought the question was too personal.

He slammed on the brakes, and she lurched forward, the seat belt restraining her. Her pounding heart could've burst from her chest and hit the windshield.

A few feet ahead a dozen or more wild turkeys excitedly darted here and there, trying to make it across the highway.

"Sorry about that," Spencer said, focused on the rearview mirror.

She stared down at the protective hand that had landed high on her belly, just under her breasts, and wondered if he even knew it was there. The jacket was too thick for her to actually feel much pressure from his palm. But there was no convincing her out-of-control heart of that.

"I'm glad you saw them in time," she said evenly and stayed perfectly still.

He turned to look at her and smoothly withdrew his hand. "You okay?"

"Fine." She stared at the poor confused-looking birds. Their numbers had doubled, and yet even more of them emerged from the scrubby brush bordering the road. "Good Lord, there's a whole—I guess you'd call it a flock?"

"Or rafter. Both are correct. See that tom?"

She looked to see where he was pointing and spotted a bird that was larger and more colorful than the others. "You mean the big testy one making all the noise?"

"A gobble can be heard up to a mile away. He's likely communicating with the rest of his harem."

Erin sent him a sideways glance. "Harem?"

"That's what they're called. Toms aren't monogamous."

"Okay." She nodded, laughing. "Now I know you're making this stuff up."

He seemed genuinely puzzled. "Why would I do that?"

"To mess with the greenhorn California girl."

"You've got wild turkeys in California, too. Alaska and Hawaii are the only states that don't have a significant population," he said, checking the rearview again. "Got a truck coming." He shifted his gaze to the parade of birds and lightly tapped his horn. "You hens need to hurry it up."

The frightened turkeys scattered every which way. A few took flight, which was pretty cool to see close up.

Once Erin was satisfied they were mostly out of danger, she said in a deep mocking voice, "That tom better keep his women in line."

With a small smile, Spencer hit the gas, and the truck quickly accelerated.

"Oh, Tom," Erin continued dramatically with a hand to her chest. "Our hero. You saved us."

Spencer's concerned look was just as phony as her punchy performance. "Do I need to take you to a hospital?"

She batted her eyelashes at him, and he actually laughed.

"And that's why I work behind the camera and not in front of it." Sighing, she glanced back to make sure all the turkeys had cleared the highway. Then she resettled in the comfy leather seat and tugged the jacket more snugly around her. She felt weird, kind of restless, but she didn't know why. Sure, she was alone with a superhot guy and had to keep her hands to herself, but other than that, everything was just peachy. "How in the world do you know all that stuff? You into trivia?"

"Nah. I was curious about them. Nowadays you can find just about anything online."

"I wish I had the option when I was a kid. I always had a million questions. Apparently I debunked the whole concept of Santa Claus when I was five. Our neighbors voted to ban me from the playground after all their kids went home crying."

A grin tugged at his mouth. "Now, why doesn't that surprise me?"

"Oh, come on. We had no fireplace or chimney, our roof was sloped with no place for a sleigh to land. And some old, fat guy was supposed to make it to every kid's house in one night?" She shrugged. "I was precocious," she said. "And persistent."

"Is that a warning?"

"Just stating the facts." Her phone rang. It was Jason. A call instead of a text? Not good.

Damn.

Why couldn't it be one of his flunkies? Easy to put them off. Damn, damn, damn. She still wasn't ready to talk to him. And definitely not in front of Spencer.

She let the call go to voice mail and waited to see if he left a message.

"Should I pull over so you can talk in private?"

"It's the director, and I'm not ready to..." *Admit*

defeat? No. Absolutely not. She looked up and smiled. "But thanks for offering."

"Is that the guy responsible for us not having sex?" Spencer asked, startling a laugh out of her. "Maybe *I* should talk to him."

"I should let you. I'd love to see you guys square off." Erin allowed herself a moment to enjoy this new relaxed version of Spencer. Before she tumbled headlong back to reality. It really was an impossible situation. "This stinks."

"Which part?"

"All of it," she said with a heartfelt sigh that seemed to make him tense. "The part we're not supposed to talk about today, and the other thing we definitely can't do…"

His mouth tightened, but he stayed focused on the road. She wasn't trying to manipulate him into giving in, but if that was what he thought, nothing she could do about it.

"Thanks for today," she said when she saw they were coming up on Main Street. "I enjoyed the ride and meeting Matt and Rachel."

"It doesn't have to end yet." He gave her a lazy smile. And more heart palpitations. "How about we go check out the new steak house?"

6

THE RESTAURANT DIDN'T open until five, so they ended up at Marge's Diner. The place was dead. The only other customer was a small hunched man sitting on a black vinyl stool at the old-fashioned counter.

The young woman refilling his coffee looked up and stopped pouring midstream when they walked in.

Spencer fought back a sigh and nodded to her and the man.

The waitress gave him a curious smile. Her face lit up at seeing Erin. "Hey, I heard you were back in town." She hurriedly topped off the white mug and wiped her hands on her apron.

"Yep. Got in yesterday morning. I can't believe how much has changed in three months."

"Erin?" The man twisted around, eyes narrowed in his weathered face.

"Hi, Myron." Erin gave him a smile. "How's the leg?"

"Doing good for now. It only acts up when it's cold."

"Are you kidding?" she said, shivering. "It's freezing out there."

The waitress—Karen, according to her name tag—

eyed Spencer's jacket engulfing Erin, then looked at him. "Hi."

"Afternoon," he said, then continued past the row of booths along the window overlooking Main Street to a table in the back corner.

Since the steak house wasn't open, Spencer should've let the matter of dinner drop. It would've been easy enough to do. Erin had even reminded him that he was supposed to get back to Shadow Creek. But she'd looked disappointed, and for whatever absurd reason he couldn't begin to understand, he hadn't wanted to let her down.

A minute later she joined him at the table, bringing menus with her. "Sorry about that," she said, her breasts thrusting against the fabric of her hoodie as she shrugged out of his jacket. "I guess I shouldn't have worn this in here."

"Why not?"

She hung it on the extra chair and took the seat opposite him. "Word spreads fast and loose in Blackfoot Falls. They'll probably have us engaged by the end of the day."

Spencer didn't doubt it, but he'd never paid any attention to gossip. He just didn't like being put on the spot with nosy questions. "I'm not worried about it," he said.

"I know how much your privacy means to you."

"People will gossip regardless of whether or not they know the truth about someone."

"Good point. I've never lived in a small town, but it's like that in the movie business, too. The stunt people hang together, and the camera crew has their own thing going on… That's human nature, I guess." Her lips twitched into a wry smile. "It makes scouting not seem so bad. Not that it stops people from talking. I'm like you, though. I don't give it a thought."

She picked up a menu, and while she studied the selections, he studied her. She had a cute habit of wrinkling her nose and nibbling on the corner of her mouth when she found something of interest.

In her black hoodie, with her messy hair and unmade-up face, she looked cute but not what most people would call a beauty. But one look at her intelligent brown eyes and the sound of that husky voice, and the pendulum swung from wholesome to downright sexy.

She glanced up and caught him staring.

Spencer didn't pretend he was doing otherwise. "What do you think people say about you?"

"You mean, if they were talking behind my back?"

He nodded.

"Hmm…" She paused. "That I'm smart, ambitious, stubborn, I work too hard, and that despite the odds, I might even succeed in this crazy, heartless business." She sighed. "Oh, and it's been mentioned that I might be more patient if I got laid once in a while."

Spencer grinned at her deadpan delivery. "I can help with that."

"Gee, thanks. I've had other offers. See, the only thing that would really help is if certain people would stop acting like self-aggrandizing, entitled idiots without a single rational brain cell and start using their damn—"

Karen had walked up and caught most of the mini rant. She blinked at Erin. "Um, did you need another minute?"

"Please," Erin said sweetly. "Coffee would be great, though."

"Decaf?" The waitress sounded almost hopeful as she set down glasses of water.

Erin laughed. "It won't help. Give me the leaded stuff. Please."

Spencer nodded to coffee as well, and Erin returned to perusing the menu.

"Any recommendations?" he asked, anxious for her to look up so he could see her eyes so full of passion and fire.

"Yeah, one. Don't shoot your mouth off until you know the coast is clear." She lifted her chin, pressing her lips together. "I had them all fooled. They thought I was nice."

"You sure?"

"Excuse me?" Erin said with lighthearted indignation just as the door opened and a middle-aged couple walked in.

"Let's be ready to order when Karen brings our coffee," Spencer said. "And by the way, I meant a meal suggestion."

"I've only eaten here twice. The meat loaf and mashed potatoes with gravy are to die for. So is the fried chicken. I'm kind of stuck on the pot roast, though." She glanced over her shoulder at the chalkboard near the door. "Did you happen to see what the pie special is?"

His gaze caught on the soft curve of her neck and the glimpse of creamy skin between her collarbones where the hoodie's ties had loosened. Just like that, lust replaced the easy humor he'd been feeling.

She turned back to him and their eyes met.

Remembering her question, he shook his head and set the menu aside. Pie wasn't the kind of dessert he had in mind.

"I have an idea," Erin said. "If we each order something different, I'll let you taste mine, and maybe I can taste…" Her voice trailed off and ended in a quiet gasp. "That didn't come out well at all."

Hunger swept through him. A hunger food couldn't satisfy. "Sounded good to me," he said, forcing himself to relax as he watched awareness dilate her pupils.

Her gaze stayed locked with his, her right eyebrow lifting ever so slightly. His mouth curved slowly in response.

More people entered the diner. A man calling out to Erin broke the spell. She blinked and then acknowledged the cowboy with a brief wave.

Jesus. Did she know every single person in town?

Karen returned with their coffee and took their dinner order. They hadn't collaborated after all and ended up both ordering pot roast. At this point, Spencer wasn't interested in what he ate. Everything seemed to have changed in the space of a heartbeat. Sure, he'd had sex on the brain since she'd gotten into his truck this morning, but it had been tempered by occasional humor. What he felt now was pure want.

Need gnawed at him like it hadn't since before he'd left Boise. Heat spread through his lower body. He pretended to listen to Karen recite the pie and ice cream selections, but if he were quizzed later, he'd fail miserably.

Seconds after the waitress left, a stout grandmotherly type approached the table with her hands on her hips, her dark, accusing eyes on Erin. "So, you're back," she said gruffly. "I haven't seen any strangers around town taking pictures yet."

"Nice to see you, Theresa." Erin beamed at the woman. "You cut your hair. I love it."

"Do you?" She patted her short brown curls, her grumpy expression replaced with uncertainty. "I'm still getting used to it." She leaned closer. "You know, I'd been wearing that bun for over thirty years."

"Better watch out," Erin whispered. "Fellas are going to come knocking at your door."

With a laugh, the woman waved off Erin's teasing and gave Spencer a quick sizing-up. "You must be from Hollywood, too."

"No, ma'am, I'm not," he said and got to his feet.

"You should be. You're handsome enough."

Spencer had never blushed in his life, but damned if he didn't feel heat crawl up his neck. He offered his chair.

Theresa shook her head. "I'll leave you two to yourselves." To Erin she said, "Come by and have a cup of coffee with me sometime."

"I'll do that."

The woman made it several steps, then turned to wag a finger. "That don't mean I approve of your people coming here and messing up our town."

"I know." Erin grinned. "Tomorrow. I'll bring cookies."

"That'll be fine," Theresa said, nodding with approval and moving on.

Spencer reclaimed his seat. "You'd make a great politician," he muttered, watching the woman until she joined her two friends waiting in a booth.

They waved. Grudgingly he waved back.

Erin laughed. "No way. I'm too outspoken."

The words were barely out of her mouth before someone else tried to get her attention. The diner was filling up, and it seemed Erin was a mini celebrity. Not everyone was in favor of giving the movie crew run of the town, but it didn't seem to matter which side of the issue people supported. They all liked Erin.

Had he known she would attract this much attention, he never would've suggested eating here.

They managed to get through their meal in relative peace. After arguing over the check, he paid the waitress, and they stepped out into the brisk fall air. Wind chill had driven the temperature down a good ten degrees.

Erin turned to say something when a violent shiver shook her slim shoulders.

"Come on," he said, holding up his jacket for her. "Your teeth are chattering."

Stubborn woman. She'd already refused, despite his repeated assurance he didn't give a damn about how it looked.

"Okay," she said, turning to give him her back, and then sighing as the warm fleece settled over her shoulders. His fingers brushed her hand when they both tried to free her hair at the same time.

His juvenile reaction to her touch warned that spending time with her might be a mistake. This was sad. He really hadn't understood just how hard up he was for sex. Maybe he should accept it as a sign he was starting to heal. Not his hand and wrist. They were fine, or at least as good as they'd ever be. Emotionally, though…

Hell, who was he kidding? He just wasn't there yet. Perhaps acceptance was the best he could hope for.

"Since you paid for dinner, you have to let me treat you to a round at the Watering Hole. Or the Full Moon Saloon. The place is new but probably noisier and more crowded."

Spencer sighed. He wouldn't have minded having a drink if he didn't think they'd be interrupted every five minutes. Although, considering his body's hair trigger, that might be a good thing.

He followed her gaze. The Watering Hole was closer,

with only two trucks parked in front. He knew how quickly that could change.

"It shouldn't get crowded until later. But if people annoy us, we can just leave," she said, taking his arm and steering him toward the bar.

"You don't have to buy me a drink."

Her arm curled around his, and while he experienced a mild jolt, he wasn't gritting his teeth to keep from jumping her bones.

"I'm supposed to be schmoozing you."

"It's not in your budget."

"How do you know?"

"You eat Twinkies for breakfast."

"Which frees up my discretionary money for schmoozing."

Spencer shook his head. "Drinks won't get me to change my mind," he said. "I don't care if you ordered a five-hundred-dollar bottle of champagne."

"Oh, well, we won't be testing that theory." She pressed closer as they crossed Main. No doubt she was merely seeking warmth, but feeling the side of her breast against his arm stirred up far too many intriguing possibilities. "Just to be clear, when does our agreement expire?"

"Are you asking when you can start pestering me again?"

She nodded. "Because technically sundown signals the end of the day."

"Do you ever take no for an answer?"

She smiled up at him. "Never."

They arrived at the bar right behind another couple. The man held open the big wooden door for the two women and then nodded to Spencer. By the time he stepped inside, someone was already talking to Erin.

Damn. If he wanted any time alone with her, he'd have to take her out to Shadow Creek. Of course, Dusty would be there. Spencer would have to think of a reason to send the kid off for the evening.

The rustic bar, with its mismatched tables and chairs, wood plank flooring and corner jukebox, was exactly what he expected in a small town like Blackfoot Falls. A pretty dark-haired waitress carrying an empty pitcher emerged from the back room, where guys were playing pool. She greeted Spencer with a smile before she slipped behind the bar.

He counted six customers in the front, including the old guy bending Erin's ear. No telling how many people were in the back room, but the place was pretty quiet.

"Sorry," Erin said as she returned to his side. "How about we take that corner table?"

"After you."

She moved quickly and sat in a chair with her back to the pool players. The waitress followed—of course, Erin knew her—but fortunately, Nikki didn't linger after she took their beer orders.

Erin leaned forward, still wrapped in his jacket and gripping the lapels together at her throat. "Do you want your jacket back?"

"Do you mean now?" he asked. "Or ever?"

"Hmm." Her lips twitched. "Let me think about that."

He stared at the tiny dimple forming at the corner of her mouth, wondering what the hell he was doing. After months of avoiding the town and the people in it, in the span of an hour, he'd eaten at the diner and was sitting in the local bar. Waiting for a beer. Something he rarely drank. He preferred scotch or wine.

Tilting her head to the side, she closed her eyes and

rubbed her cheek against the sherpa lining. "God, this feels amazing."

Her naturally pink lips were slightly parted. She didn't need makeup. Her skin was as smooth as satin. Flawless.

The soft sound she made was equal parts sigh and moan. Her long, silky lashes fluttered.

Jesus. She was killing him.

He had to look away.

Erin was smart. This was all part of the act. She knew exactly what she was doing.

"What is this lining called?" she asked in that damn husky voice of hers.

"Tell me something," he said, instead of answering. "What's going to happen when you tell the director you couldn't get Moonlight Mountain?"

She slowly opened her eyes and sighed as if he'd woken her from a pleasant dream. "He'll yell and cuss for a minute, or until he remembers that I never respond to his tantrums. Not favorably, anyway. Then he'll remind me of how much we all have at stake." She spoke calmly and thoughtfully, oblivious to Spencer's attempt to undermine her confidence. Or whatever it was she was playing at.

Damn her.

She paused and smiled her thanks when Nikki set down their mugs of beer before moving to another table.

"Jason can be temperamental," Erin continued. "But talk about being a politician. He'll turn right around and start stroking my ego. Assuring me he has every confidence I won't let him down. I swear the man can go on and on ad nauseam."

"Can he fire you?"

Erin took a small sip, her expression thoughtful.

"Technically, I suppose he could. But he won't. For one thing, I'm not getting paid—" She made a face. "I think I mentioned the arrangement is complicated, though not uncommon for an indie film. Anyway, the bottom line is he knows I'll do everything in my power to make the film a success." She shrugged, smiled. "That being said, it's never a good idea to piss off the director."

Spencer felt himself being drawn into her web again. Even after she'd just admitted she would be willing to do anything to ensure the film's success. But she wasn't faking the passion that flashed in her eyes. And he couldn't help but admire her unwavering persistence in keeping her dream alive despite the questionable odds.

"Erin!" A tall, grinning cowboy with a cue stick in one hand and a beer in the other came from the back room. "'Bout time you showed up. You owe me another game, darlin'."

She snorted a laugh. "The hell I do. I beat you two out of three times, fair and square. Get over it. *Darlin'*."

"Come on now." He eyed Spencer, reluctantly giving him a nod. "It ain't right leavin' a man with his head hangin'."

Two more guys appeared behind him. They both remembered Erin from her last visit and urged her to join them for a game.

She joked around with them for a minute and then got serious. "Come on, guys. Knock it off. Can't you see I'm on a date?" She glanced at Spencer with an impish gleam in her eye. "If you all keep interrupting, how am I supposed to get lucky?"

The tall cowboy snorted. "That ain't fair. You wouldn't give me one lousy chance."

The other two headed back to the pool tables.

"Nice seeing you. Goodbye," Erin said, with a shooing motion.

The man laughingly pointed his beer at Spencer as he backed up. "Dude, don't let her hustle you."

The comment seemed good-natured enough, but Spencer felt like a chump.

Hell, he was probably letting her do exactly that.

7

"I'M SORRY I embarrassed you," Erin said once they were outside and headed toward his truck.

"You didn't embarrass me, so don't worry about it."

She wished she could read him better. Something was bothering him since she'd made the joke about getting lucky. So, what was she supposed to think?

Spencer had adjusted his stride to accommodate her shorter legs. And he'd made a point of doing the gentlemanly thing of positioning himself between her and the street. She might've teased him about his old-fashioned manners if she wasn't already walking on thin ice. Anyway, she thought it was kind of sweet.

He stuffed his hands deep into the pocket of his jeans, and his shoulders were hunched slightly.

"Oh, God, I'm such a jerk," she said, slipping off his jacket. "Here. Take this."

"Keep it on until I drop you off."

"I can walk to the inn. It's not far, and you're going the other way." She pushed the jacket at him, but he wouldn't take it. "Fine," she said and draped it over her arm.

They walked in stubborn silence until they got to

his truck. She couldn't understand why he'd insisted on driving her when his mood had clearly plummeted. She stood at the passenger door waiting for him to unlock it.

"What are you doing?" He was just staring at her, his hands stuffed in his pockets.

She frowned at him. "You're the one who insisted on giving me a ride."

He slowly nodded. "Wrong one."

"What?"

He glanced up ahead as if the sidewalk held some huge significance. When she didn't move, he walked over and took her hand. "This isn't my truck."

He led her a few feet to another silver truck parked in front.

"Why didn't you say something?"

"I did." Clearly trying not to laugh, he hadn't released her hand yet.

"Yeah, I'm sure you've never made a mistake in your life, Mr. Perfect."

"Oh, I've made plenty." His grip tightened. "This might even be another one," he murmured, lowering his head.

Their lips touched. Slowly. Deceptively gentle.

Something so sweet and controlled shouldn't have set off a five-alarm response in her.

Without disturbing the kiss, Spencer took the jacket from her and put it back around her shoulders. He gave the front a light tug, and she fell half a step forward, right up against his strong, solid body. One palm landed flat on his chest. His lips were warm and persuasive in their subtle movements. She felt the tip of his tongue probe the corner of her mouth. How could she even think about kissing him right here, in the middle of

Main Street? The rough sound of an engine revved closer, but she parted her lips for him, anyway.

Their tongues had barely touched when Spencer drew away. “Come on, let’s get out of here,” he said and used the remote to unlock the doors.

She was shivering by the time she climbed into his truck. Not from the cold. She was still wrapped warmly in his jacket. She had no idea what came next, but she had about ten seconds to figure out what she wanted to do before he slid behind the wheel.

Without a word he started the engine, and soon they were headed toward The Boarding House. Erin had been blessed with the gift of gab. But she couldn’t think of a damn thing to say. She could still taste him on her lips. A block from the inn she gathered the bag she’d left on the floorboard. The porch was lit, and as they got closer, she noticed the carved pumpkins on the steps. And then there they went.

She swung her gaze to Spencer. “You just passed—”

“I know.” He shot her a look. “You okay with that?”

“Sure,” she said slowly. “Where are we going?”

“I’m not sure.”

“Oh, well—” She swallowed, searching for one of the trusty quips she usually kept on the tip of her tongue. But she couldn’t focus. She was too absorbed by the memory of his tongue grazing her lips.

“I’m not done kissing you,” he said as they passed the filling station, leaving the town behind them.

Dammit.

Her body jumped back into overdrive. She didn’t dare say a word. Not until she could settle long enough to think. Staring at his strong profile didn’t help. His jaw and nose were too perfect. After working in Hollywood for so long, she would’ve thought she’d be immune to "pretty men." Her gaze moved to his hands. To his long lean fingers. She'd bet anything he knew just how to touch a woman.

None of this was helping. It only stoked the ache inside her, pushing her to ignore reason. Maybe she was being too guarded about the sex issue. Too many Neanderthals in Hollywood still used it as a bargaining chip. And if smart, competent women rose among the ranks, remarks were still made about how they got there. In this day and age. Unbelievable, and yet true. And so, yeah, she was careful about mixing sex with business.

It startled her when he pulled over on the narrow shoulder. Nothing was there but trees and brush in the semidarkness. Letting the truck idle, he turned to face her. "You're quiet."

"Do you have any idea how many people would pay to have me shut up?"

It was light enough that she could see his faint smile. "Do you want to go back?" he asked, resting his arm on the back of her seat but not touching her.

"Not necessarily." Her mouth had gone dry. God, she sounded like a frog. "Then I'd have to return your jacket."

"Not necessarily," he echoed, and she grinned. "You want to go to Shadow Creek?"

"Your place?" Now her voice had risen three octaves.

"Last I checked."

"We're going in the wrong direction."

"Easy enough to rectify," he said, touching her hair.

"What I said at the Watering Hole was a joke. You get that, right? Because we're not getting lucky." She paused for a quick swallow. "I mean, I'm not. You might. Just not with me."

"I know." He leaned forward. His hand slid around

to cradle her nape, and before she could withdraw or protest, their lips touched.

Erin might've met him halfway when she really should've told him to stop. This would only lead to trouble. But with each light nibble, she cared less and less. He pushed his fingers into her hair, caressing her scalp, while he trailed damp kisses along her jaw. She shifted slightly, and when he pressed his mouth against hers, harder this time, she welcomed him inside. His tongue stroked hers before sweeping the inside of her mouth. He didn't taste like beer. He should have, but he didn't. Erin hoped she didn't, either.

She didn't know what to do with her hands. She was clinging to his jacket so tightly her fingers started to ache. Before she could decide, the headlights from an oncoming vehicle swept the cab of the truck. The beam hit them only briefly, but it was enough for them to break apart.

Shocked that she was practically sitting on the console, Erin shrank back to her side.

"I guess I could've found a better place to pull over," Spencer said ruefully. "Though I'd only planned to talk."

"Uh-huh. Sure."

"You'd already made your position clear."

Erin laughed. "Yes, I did. And that hasn't changed."

Her cell rang. It was Lila's ringtone. Tough. She'd have to leave a message. Erin pulled the phone out of her pocket meaning to shut off the ringer but accepted the call by mistake.

"Damn," she muttered, giving Spencer an apologetic shrug. She'd get rid of Lila quickly. "What!?"

"Jeez. You don't have to yell," Lila said. "Hey, I

meant to ask, have you found a date for the awards dinner yet?"

"No. Why are you— Who said I'm taking a date?" She glanced at Spencer, who was checking something on his phone. But of course he could hear every word. "Look, I can't talk. I'll call you later."

"You sound off. Where are you?"

"Do I ask where you are every minute?"

"Um, pretty much. Why are you being so weird?"

"I'm hanging up. We'll talk later."

"Oh, my God, you're with—"

Erin disconnected and switched the phone off before cramming it back into her pocket. She sat quietly, waiting until he looked up, before she said, "Sorry, it was my friend Lila."

"No problem. It gave me a chance to reply to a text." He rested a hand on the wheel. "We can't sit out here. I can drop you off back at The Boarding House." He paused, searching her face in the semidarkness. "I'm assuming that's what you want."

She wanted him to kiss her again. Though she was still a bit shaky from the last one, and anyway, hadn't she decided kissing only meant trouble? Plus, he apparently was no longer considering taking her to Shadow Creek, or he would've mentioned it as an option.

Erin held back a sigh. "Sure, the inn would be fine. I have calls to make and strategies to devise."

His mouth curved in a slight smile as he put the truck in Drive, but he didn't even try to talk her out of it. So maybe he'd changed his mind. It was for the best. After he made a smooth U-turn, they drove in silence until the lights from the gas station became visible.

Spencer spoke first. "You kept your word and didn't

pressure me about Moonlight Mountain," he said. "I appreciate that."

"Yeah, well, tomorrow's another day."

He gave her a look that was far from amused. "Here I was going to invite you to dinner at the ranch tomorrow."

Erin studied his handsome profile. "And now you're not?"

"Depends."

"Seriously? We can't talk about the mountain?"

He shook his head.

She stewed for a minute, unable to take her eyes off him. Part of his problem was that he was just too damn good-looking. He was probably used to getting his way with women. So maybe it was best she had no more social contact with him. But then she risked never seeing him again. He'd kick her off his property. He'd done it before.

All he really wanted was sex and for her to stop pressuring him. In truth, she had a horrible feeling this was one battle she would likely lose. She couldn't go down without more of a fight, though. Giving up wasn't in her DNA.

"Will Dusty be there tomorrow?" she asked as he pulled the truck up to the inn's walkway.

The corners of his mouth barely twitched yet somehow conveyed his self-satisfaction. "I think he has plans."

Erin took some small comfort in knowing his smugness was misguided. She didn't know why she'd asked, but it had nothing to do with them getting naked. After waiting a few moments with her hand resting on the door handle, she asked, "Am I invited or not?"

"You know the conditions."

"Fine." She gritted her teeth to keep from saying something regrettable. "What time?"

"How about 7:00?"

She thought country people tended to eat earlier. Maybe he wanted to get rid of Dusty first. Ha. He'd see how far that got him. "Sounds good. Can I bring anything?"

Spencer shook his head. "It won't be anything fancy. Want me to pick you up?"

"I know the way." She grabbed her bag off the floor and lifted the door handle.

"Wait."

Reluctantly, she glanced back at him. And realized she'd been about to abscond with his jacket. "Oh, shit, sorry." Dropping the bag, she leaned forward and did a little shimmy that sent the heavy suede jacket sliding off her shoulders onto the seat.

"You trying to hustle me, Erin?" His deep, raspy murmur heated her skin, spread through her chest, then pooled low in her belly. "Is that it?" he asked, lifting his gaze from the vicinity of her breasts to stare into her eyes.

What the hell was he talking about? She blinked, trying to pull herself out of the haze of confusion mixed with desire. He came into focus, and the look of pure lust on his face astonished her. Guys just didn't look at her that way. So who was hustling whom?

"I should ask you the same question," she said and dodged his touch when he tried to stroke her cheek.

"I have no reason to hustle you."

"You want sex."

"So do you," he said, his voice still maddeningly low and raspy and somehow trying to trick her.

She didn't bother denying it. "I'm not hustling you.

If I were, we'd be screwing each other's brains out by now."

Spencer laughed, and even that sounded sexy…until it ended in a groan. "Instead, you're trying to kill me."

"I have no idea what you're talking about," she said, but then his gaze briefly swept the front of her hoodie, and she remembered the little shimmy. It hadn't been for his benefit. That was just how she undressed. Besides, it wasn't as if she had large breasts. "Men are weird."

"I won't argue." He stared absently out the windshield into the growing darkness. With a resigned sigh, he turned to look at her, a helpless expression on his face. "I can't stop thinking about this," he said and reached for her.

ERIN SCOOTED CLOSER and eagerly responded to his kiss. If she hadn't, or if she'd told him to screw off, he didn't know what he would've done. Stop, of course, but after that?

He told himself to go slowly and not give her a reason to push him away. Her soft, plump lips made it easy for him to linger. So smooth and silky. Just like her hair and the warm skin behind her neck.

Shit.

It didn't make sense. This pull he felt. He didn't understand why he wanted her so damn much. Why he'd purposely driven through town hoping to see her. This wasn't like him. For ten months he'd gone out of his way to avoid people. Jesus, and he'd invited her to the ranch for dinner.

Sure, she was attractive, intelligent, ambitious, outgoing. That was the sort of woman he was attracted to, but this was on a whole other level. What was it about Erin that made her so different? He couldn't put his finger on it, and it was driving him crazy. If he'd had any kind of handle on this thing, he would've never come to town in the first place.

He moved on to her jaw, trailing kisses to her ear, and nibbled at the soft lobe. She liked that. Her throaty moan almost sounded like a purr, and damned if that didn't go straight to his cock. When she pressed closer, his plan to keep it slow was shot to hell.

He reclaimed her mouth, changing angles and slipping his tongue between her parted lips. She joined the dance quickly, surprising him with the intensity of her response. Each stroke of his tongue was met with unbridled enthusiasm.

He'd completely lost control over his own body. His cock pulsed against the thick denim of his jeans. Kissing wasn't enough. He wanted to touch her. Cradle the weight of her naked breasts in his palms—

Erin jerked back and shoved him away at the same time. "Damn you," she muttered. "Damn you."

He could see her heart-shaped face in the dim light. Eyes glaring, color spreading across her pale cheeks. She looked confused and angry.

"It was only a kiss," he said quietly.

She pressed her lips together and opened the door. He had a feeling her anger was directed more at herself than him. Hell, he wasn't happy with himself, either.

After she slid out and before she could slam the door, he said, "Tomorrow night?" He half expected her to say no. Half hoped she did.

For a second she looked torn. "Yes," she said, the word like a curse. "Happy now?"

Good thing she spun toward the inn and didn't catch his smile. He waited, though, watching her take long, quick strides to the porch and race up the steps. She disappeared inside without a single glance back.

Spencer winced and adjusted his jeans, something he should've done before now. He still didn't get it. What was it about her that had him restless and second-guessing himself?

Was it her scent? Mostly she smelled like vanilla, which he liked a lot, although it wasn't anything special. Damn, he knew better than to let his testosterone do the thinking. More proof he wasn't thinking clearly. An artificial scent wouldn't likely be responsible, but it was possible that pheromones could be what had turned him into an idiot.

It was as good an explanation as anything else. He wasn't reaching. There was research to support the theory. Not everyone in the scientific community believed it. But he specialized in animals and not humans, and he knew how much scent played a part in their world. So he tried to keep an open mind.

Erin wasn't alone in her insatiable curiosity. He always wanted to know the science behind everything. It was the way his mind worked. His love of both science and animals was the reason he'd gone through so many years of veterinary school.

Sighing, Spencer put the truck in Drive. Nowadays, it only depressed him to think all those years had been for nothing.

8

ERIN REGRETTED NOT running over to the Full Moon Saloon last night. She studied the photo she'd just taken of the outside. The eighty-year-old wood-front structure wasn't bad, but it was the quaint, old-time feel of the inside that Jason was going to love. And God only knew how much she needed the bonus points.

The bar opened at 6:00, according to the sign on the door. That gave her enough time to dash in before driving out to Spencer's for dinner.

The thought of seeing him again gave her the jitters. Her juvenile reaction was so stupid she could hardly stand it. And yet this was the third time she'd had to stop, breathe deeply and force herself to remember it was no big deal. Because nothing was going to happen.

Not tonight.

Or tomorrow night.

Or any night.

In a few months, after they'd wrapped up filming, then *maybe*...if she had time to come back, they could hook up.

Oh, hell. By then he would've forgotten all about her. She'd be a moron to think otherwise.

Lack of sleep was the problem. Going to bed frustrated was one thing, but to have her vibrator conk out last night, of all nights? Unacceptable. Just plain cruel. Fate sucked.

Her own stupid brain hadn't helped, either. Of course she had to lie awake listing all the things she should've said to him. Just about anything would've been more eloquent than *damn you*. She was usually witty and quick with her comebacks.

She crossed Main to get a wider shot of the Full Moon and the bakery next door. She held up the camera and was setting up the shot when she saw a tall blonde woman stop at the bar's door and pull out some keys.

Erin scratched the photo and made it back across the street just as the woman stepped inside and was closing the big wooden door.

"Excuse me," Erin said, sticking out her foot and hoping she didn't lose it under the thick, heavy door.

The blonde gave her a quick smile and said, "We don't open until six."

"I know. Are you the owner?"

"Yes," she said with obvious reluctance.

"Erin Murphy." She stuck her hand out. "With Crazy Coyote Productions. I'm hoping Sadie—Mayor Thompson—has mentioned the film we'll be shooting in the area."

"Oh, sure." She opened the door wider and shook Erin's hand. "I'm Mallory. Come in," she said, stepping aside and letting Erin pass before locking the door behind them.

Erin glanced around at the plank floor and the same scarred oak bar that had been there before when she'd checked out the place. The old-fashioned jukebox was new and so was the stage and dance floor. They didn't stand out, though. Care had been taken to keep the old-time feel of the room.

She moved in for a better look at the assorted wood signs hanging on the mirror behind the bar and on the walls. They'd been roughly crafted, advertising things like *sarsaparillas* and *beer for two bits*. "Are those originals?"

"Yep," Mallory said. "Hand-carved in the early 1900s from what I was told."

"Very cool. I love how you've kept the rustic feel. I saw the place three months ago when it was vacant." Spotting the mechanical bull in the back, Erin grinned. She'd need a couple tequila shots first.

Suddenly she remembered what Matt had said about Spencer being a rodeo guy. Oh, she was definitely dragging him in here.

"I had a scare a week after I opened." Mallory nodded at the stage. "An electrical fire started right there. I lost tables and chairs, and I had to replace the new dance floor I'd just put in. And of course the stage had to be rebuilt. There was some smoke damage… But all and all, I was pretty lucky."

"Yeah, I would say so." Erin honestly couldn't see a single telltale sign.

"I don't know what I would've done without the people around here. Folks I'd never met pitched in to help clean up and rebuild. Most of those wood plaques were dug out of their attics and garages." Mallory shook her head as if she still didn't quite believe what had happened. "I'd just moved here. I'm from California."

"Oh, me, too. Which part?"

"Southern Cal. Valencia."

"We were practically neighbors. I grew up in Santa Clarita, right near Six Flags."

"Wow! Yeah." Mallory grinned. "I knew you worked in Hollywood, but that doesn't mean anything. You could've been from anywhere." She slipped behind the bar. "How about something to drink? I've got cola and juice if you don't want any alcohol."

"I think I'm fine. Too much coffee, actually," she said, pressing a hand to her jittery stomach. It wasn't the coffee. She'd just caught another glimpse of the mechanical bull and remembered the casual way Spencer had popped into her head.

"Listen, I don't mean to keep you, I have a contract with the town that includes—"

"No worries." Mallory smiled. "Sadie explained everything before I leased the place."

"Oh, good. We haven't spoken since July, but I figured she would've handled it. I honestly can't say if the director will shoot footage in here or not, but we won't interfere with your business hours."

"I'm closed on Sundays and Mondays if that helps."

Erin gave her a wry smile. "You might want to rethink that when the film crew hits town. A lot of them like to drink when they aren't working. You'll probably want to double your booze orders, too."

Mallory nodded. "I owned a bar in Valencia. My customers were mostly stuntmen and a few wranglers. I'll be ready for them."

"Perfect," Erin said, relieved. If only Spencer had been this accommodating. "Do you mind if I take some pictures to send to the director?"

"Go right ahead," Mallory said, gesturing broadly. "Let me know if you need anything."

What a great score. Erin had a feeling Jason would prefer using the Full Moon over the Watering Hole. Or maybe he'd shoot scenes in both bars. The Watering

Hole had its own brand of charm. That Mallory knew the drill and Erin liked her was a bonus.

She quickly finished snapping photos, and after promising to stop in for a drink soon, she left Mallory to do her inventory.

Outside the air was brisk, but the sky was clear and the sun was bright. Erin stayed out of the shade to help keep warm. Damn, she missed Spencer's jacket. Her poor hoodie just wasn't up to the task. Main Street was dead, and she had no trouble navigating the sidewalk while reviewing the pictures. She stopped after deciding which ones Jason would like and sent them to his phone.

According to Lila, who'd mercilessly grilled Erin earlier, they were filming in a remote area that had poor cell service today. Thank God. Erin had enough to be nervous about. She didn't need Jason calling to yell at her. That would only piss her off, and the two of them had been known to go at it tooth and nail on occasion.

Yawning, she wondered if she should take more pictures of the new motel or let it wait and take a short nap instead. Before she'd made up her mind, her cell rang.

Lila? Again? She probably had more questions about Spencer.

Sighing, Erin started walking in the direction of the inn. Definitely nap first.

She accepted the call and said, "Uncle Sam needs someone like you. You'd make one hell of a good interrogator."

"Yeah, I figured you'd answer for her."

Erin froze. "Jason?"

"What's wrong, Murphy? Aren't you happy to hear from me?"

"I'd rather eat liver." The stupid thought grossed her out. "What do you want?"

"Shit," Jason said, drawing out the word. "You actually have the balls to ask me that?"

"Did you not get the voice mail I left you?"

"I got it." He paused briefly. "Move that goddamn track! I can see from here I'm not going to get the depth of feel I need. Where's the dolly grip?" Obviously he wasn't talking to her, but his loud screech nearly shattered her eardrum. "Damn morons," he muttered. "You there?"

"Don't ever yell into the phone like that again." Erin noticed a woman with her kid admiring the Halloween window decorations as they strolled toward her. She never swore in public. Not the real bad words, anyway. But Jason could make her crazy, so she stepped into a narrow alley…just in case. "I was very clear that I had no news and I'd call you when I knew something."

"I want that mountain, Erin. I can't see the ending any other way. You know what it looks like in the golden hour, and none of the other mountains have that peak I need. It says something. I'm not just being a goddamn auteur. You said you'd get it. If I can't trust you to do this, then what?"

"I understand. I do," she said, doing her best to keep her voice low and even. "You know I do. But I need more time."

"Offer him more money."

"You complained about the last figure I quoted him."

Jason let out a string of curses.

She held the phone away until he finished. "Not everyone is motivated by money. I'm working on Hunt, but it's taking some time."

"We don't have time."

"Yeah, well, we don't have money, either." She cringed at her slip. No use reminding him they were over budget.

"Look, those two alternatives I gave you really aren't bad. Maybe you should start thinking about using one of them from a different angle."

His silence was as deafening as his shouting. "Don't tell me you've given up."

"Me? You know better. But if you're concerned about the timing, you need to consider other options. This guy really doesn't want us on his property. I haven't figured out what it's going to take—"

"Christ, sleep with him if you have to. I'll send Lila down there. Make it a threesome. The guy won't know what hit him."

Erin's shock was surpassed only by her anger. "What did you say?" she asked in a deceptively calm voice.

"I was joking."

She wished she could believe that. They went back ten years. She knew he was stressed, but she expected better from him. "Actually, Hunt is more your type. How about you make a quick overnight trip?"

"It was a goddamn joke." Jason sighed, his voice muffled. He had a habit of rubbing his face when put on the spot. "I have faith in you. If anyone can lead a horse to water and make him drink, it's you."

Erin couldn't help it; she laughed. Jason had been here too long. He wasn't the type to get folksy.

"If it turns out he wants more money, give it to him. Use your discretion." He paused. "Just remember, you have a lot at stake yourself."

A chill passed through her. What he'd said was true. But it was the underlying message in his tone that made the hair on the back of her neck stand up. "Are you threatening me, Jason?"

"Lighten up. It was a reminder."

As if she needed one. "Don't you dare dangle the

AD job over me. I've already earned that spot, and you damn well know it." She heard background chatter and realized he was talking to someone else. Anger raged through her. Yeah, they were both tired. But this was bullshit. "Jason?" she said evenly and waited for him.

"Yeah?"

"Fu—" She stuck her head out of the alley. The mom and kid were closing in. "Screw you," she ground out at the same instant she noticed Dusty from the corner of her eye.

He was standing on the sidewalk a few feet away, waiting for her, it appeared, and had probably heard everything she'd said.

DUSTY STOOD AT the door to the mudroom, checking to see if he'd used the right holes to button his good shirt. "You sure you don't mind if I get home late?" Dusty asked for the second time since he'd showered and put on too much aftershave.

"You're nineteen," Spencer said, "and I'm not your father. Come home whenever you want."

Spencer knew he sounded grouchy. Part of his edgy mood stemmed from guilt. He deliberately hadn't told Dusty that Erin was coming over. The kid still had a thing for her, and Spencer had discouraged him from asking her out. Easy to misread his motives, even though Spencer honestly hadn't set his sights on Erin.

The other thing eating at him was plain ol' jealousy. Dusty was going to get laid tonight, and Spencer had nothing but a hand job to look forward to. And because life was rarely fair, it would be his own hand doing the deed.

Dusty hadn't mentioned the reason for his trip to

Kalispell, but he didn't have to. He'd scrubbed his boots and combed his hair.

Spencer got a beer out of the fridge and took a quick look at the clock. Hell, he wished the kid would just leave. Erin was supposed to arrive in thirty minutes.

"See, I wouldn't have asked except we still got a lot of fence to mend before it snows, and when I say I'm coming home late, what I mean is—"

"Oh, hell." He twisted the cap off the bottle. "Go. Have a good time. I won't start worrying for a week. How's that?"

Dusty frowned. "Maybe you should come with me. Bridgette's got a real pretty friend—"

Spencer nearly choked on his first sip.

"They're both legal."

"Yeah, thanks. No."

With a shrug, Dusty turned to leave, then stopped. "By the way, I ran into Erin in town."

Spencer set the bottle down. "Today?"

Nodding, Dusty watched as Spencer flexed his hand. The cold often affected it; nothing noteworthy there. Dusty knew that because he'd worked for him back in Boise. "I think her boss is really pissed at her."

"Did Erin tell you that?"

Dusty shook his head. "I didn't mean to, but I kind of overheard her talking to him."

"Jason's here?"

Dusty stared at him. "Is that her boss's name?"

With a casual shrug, Spencer picked up his beer. "Jason Littleton is the director. I assume he's Erin's boss."

"How do you know—" Dusty's expression slid from confusion to hope. "Did you change your mind? Because

Erin's right, none of them movie people would have to come anywhere near the house or the—"

Spencer held a hand up for silence. "No, I haven't changed my mind."

"I figured you must've signed the contract," Dusty said, eyeing him with curiosity, "being that you know the director's name and all."

Clearly Erin hadn't said anything about their excursion yesterday or about dinner tonight. Spencer had a good reason for keeping quiet. He wondered about hers. As for Dusty, he wasn't hiding anything. The kid was as guileless as they came.

He was curious, though, and so busy staring that he hadn't budged. "Tell me the truth, Doc, wouldn't you feel god-awful if she got fired over it?"

"She's not going to get fired." Spencer walked toward the mudroom, hoping to get Dusty moving. "And we talked about you calling me Doc."

"Sorry. It slipped."

"You have enough cash on you?"

Dusty stepped back, frantically patting his pockets. "Dang it. I've got my wallet but forgot my money clip. Must be on the dresser. Good thing you said something."

Blocking his path, Spencer reached into his back pocket. "Here," he said, pulling a hundred-dollar bill and three twenties out of his wallet. "Consider it an early Halloween bonus."

Dusty's laugh ended as his eyes widened at the money. "No shit?"

"No shit."

"Thanks, Doc. I mean, Boss." Dusty swiftly snatched the cash as if he expected Spencer to change his mind. "I'll see you later," he said, grabbing his jacket off a peg. "Make that tomorrow."

Spencer nodded and vaguely heard the door to the garage open and close. His thoughts kept circling back to Erin and why she'd chosen to keep their rendezvous quiet. Did it mean she was warming up to the idea of them having sex? She'd be more careful about giving folks room to speculate. It wouldn't be enough that she and Spencer knew sex wasn't being used to negotiate. And he wouldn't blame her for being extra cautious.

The thought was gaining more ground in his brain. It was a logical assumption. Or else his extended abstinence was making him delusional. Hell, he was going with the happy ending.

Just maybe he wouldn't have to settle for rosy palm and her five sisters.

9

RELIEVED TO SEE all the floodlights Spencer had left on, Erin drove slowly down the long driveway and parked her car where she could see solid ground. No more mud baths for her. The memory of her grand entrance that first day made her want to turn around and lay tracks straight to LA.

She climbed out of the car, barely acknowledging the pink bakery box sitting on the passenger seat. Her gaze caught on the ethereal, silvery glow that shimmered around Moonlight Mountain. Beautiful, stunning…words seemed inadequate to describe what the rising moon was doing to its namesake.

The sky was clear. A few clouds clung to the Rockies in the distance. The first stars had twinkled into view. But the mountain took center stage. Accustomed to Hollywood creations, it was easy to forget Mother Nature needed no help to work her own magic.

Erin had no idea how long she'd been standing there, when she heard the front door open.

Spencer walked onto the spacious wraparound porch and then down the steps. With his hair combed back and wearing a blue Western-cut shirt tucked into dark jeans, he was almost as gorgeous as his mountain. "Something wrong?" he asked as he approached.

"Just admiring the view." She smiled, annoyed at the flutter in her tummy. "The mountain, not you."

He looked startled, then laughed.

"It's so beautiful out here. Clear skies. No noise. The air is clean…"

He'd almost reached her when he stopped to follow her gaze. "It's something, all right," he agreed. "The moment I saw the place I knew I was going to buy it. But I hated the name Moonlight Mountain. I figured the locals would give me a load of grief if I changed it and decided it wasn't worth the hassle."

"*I* would've given you a load of grief."

He turned to her with a raised brow. "Sweetheart, you've given me a lot worse than that."

"Oddly, you're not the first person to tell me that."

He smiled, his gaze sweeping her black skinny jeans and cream-colored sweater before coming back to her face. "You look nice," he said. "Much better than the view."

"Ah, that was sweet," she said with an equally sweet smile. "FYI—flattery won't get you laid." She caught his smirk before she ducked into the car to grab the pastries. She used the moment to breathe in deeply because, God, how was she ever going to keep her hands off him tonight? She straightened and held up the box like it was time for show-and-tell. "I brought dessert."

"Good," he said, tightening his mouth.

"Don't say it. I've already heard every joke there is."

"Got it." He held out his hand. "The wind is picking up. Let's go inside."

She gave him the box. A second later she realized he'd wanted her hand, not the pastries.

"The ground is hard," he said, watching her pick her way slowly to the porch. "No more surprises."

She also wasn't wearing those ridiculous heels. But when he again offered his hand, she gladly accepted it.

They walked up the steps together, and then he pushed the door open for her.

The inside looked different than it had the other day. A stone fireplace dominated the living room. A brown leather couch faced a pair of wing chairs, a gleaming dark wood coffee table placed between them. No carpeting at all, just hardwood floors and several large area rugs. The walls were bare, yet with a few decorative items scattered here and there, the room looked attractive and homey with a modern twist.

"Everything meet with your approval?"

"What?" She glanced over her shoulder at him standing in the doorway, waiting for her to move. "Oh," she said, stepping aside. "I hadn't seen the room from this angle. It's really nice. Love the fireplace."

"It's my favorite thing about the house. There's a smaller version in the den and another one in my bedroom."

"Wow. Yeah, that would've sold me."

"If you behave, I'll show them to you." He walked past her to the kitchen and set the box on the counter.

"Huh. You want me to behave. That's a switch." She sniffed the air. "Are you cooking?"

His brows rose. "I did invite you for dinner. Unless you have something else in mind…"

"Don't be silly." She caught a glimpse of his gloomy expression and, trying not to laugh, she turned to a fancy chess set sitting on the coffee table. "I'm looking forward to a real meal. But I gotta admit, I expected takeout or sandwiches."

"Oh, ye of little faith," he said. "The potatoes are almost done and the salad is finished. I just have to grill the steaks. Does anything in this box need to be refrigerated?"

Erin set down the silver pawn she'd picked up. "Grill, as in barbecue?" she asked as she walked over to him. "As in outside in the freezing cold?"

"Freezing?" Shaking his head, he opened the refrigerator door. "You really do need to buy a good jacket."

"I hate spending money on something I'll only use for a couple days."

Spencer swung a look at her, completely ignoring the open fridge. "You're leaving that soon?"

"Probably." She shrugged. "I should be finished here, and you said it yourself, no sense hanging around and paying for lodging." She opened the box and frowned. "Do you think it'll be okay to leave out the éclair? I always eat 'em too fast to worry about storing them."

He didn't reply. But he did take two steaks out of the fridge. "So, you've finally come to your senses and have given up on me."

"You wish." She carefully avoided looking for his reaction. She wasn't playing him, not really. Well, maybe a little. Though she preferred to think of it as psychological warfare. "What about the napoleon? Leave it out, too?"

He set down shakers of sea salt and black pepper on the gray-and-taupe countertop. "I don't understand."

"Well, since I don't know what you like, I decided to bring three different kinds—the third option in case Dusty was here."

"I was talking about you leaving." He looked adorably confused with his clean-shaven face and his blue shirt bringing out the green in his eyes.

"Oh." She gave him a bright smile. "Would you prefer I stay and annoy the hell out of you?"

He didn't look amused. "There's beer, wine, juice. Help yourself," he said and put all of his attention into seasoning the meat.

She closed the box and turned to face him, her arms folded. "Care to tell me what's wrong?"

"You ran into Dusty in town."

"I didn't say one word to him about coming here tonight."

"I know. No need to be defensive." He picked up the platter, grabbed a pair of long-handled tongs and started walking.

She followed him as he veered away from the mudroom, past the small bathroom where she'd changed clothes and down a short hall.

He led her into a room about the size of the living room, although three huge windows made it seem more spacious. Two of the walls were floor-to-ceiling bookshelves, crammed mostly with hardbacks. And there was the other fireplace he'd mentioned, except it didn't look smaller at all.

Everything was so neat and uncluttered—even the cherry desk with the laptop and stack of mail sitting on top of it. She had the sudden urge to mess things up a little bit.

"Are you coming?"

She turned toward the sound of Spencer's voice. He stood just outside, to the left of the windows, holding open a glass door she hadn't noticed. Her gaze drew to the perfect view of Moonlight Mountain.

Part of the big round moon was now visible over the peak. It gave the illusion of an iridescent silver halo against the darkening sky. What a stunning picture.

Breathtaking.

He flipped on an outside light and waited at the door for her.

"Watch your step," he said, then took her arm and guided her down three steps to a semi-covered patio.

"This is a nice surprise," she said. *If it were warmer.*

"Mind holding this for a second?"

She took the platter and tongs from him and divided her attention between the mountain and watching him uncover a massive stainless steel barbecue equipped with side burners and other fancy doodads.

The house blocked the cold wind whipping through the trees in front, making it more pleasant in their little corner. That wasn't to say she would've chosen to barbecue.

"Where's the charcoal?"

"It's gas," he said and turned a dial. A flame appeared like magic.

"I thought cowboys like to sit around the campfire and cook whatever they caught on a stick."

He took the platter from her and set it next to the grill, then nodded at something hidden under a large tarp. "There's a fire pit and table under there if you'd prefer to dine alfresco."

"First, you're completely insane. It's freezing. Second, dine alfresco? Who *are* you? I'd bet a hundred bucks 80 percent of the guys around here have no idea what that means."

She expected a laugh, maybe even a comeback, but he just turned to transfer the steaks to the grill. Something seemed off with him.

More stars had shown themselves. She stared up at the dots of light, blinking to make them twinkle, just like she had as a kid, lying on the grass, making up stories about aliens and faraway worlds.

Her gaze returned to the mountain, so tall and regal standing all by itself, refusing to be cowed by the famous Rockies off to the west. It took only minutes of looking away from the jagged ridges and sloping planes to see how much the rising moon had changed the landscape.

The moonlight that had glistened benevolently now cast eerie shadows full of mystery. Erin remembered taking the photos that had sold Jason on using the mountain for the final scene. How could it have been only three months ago? Somehow the mountain looked different than it had back then.

More peaceful.

Untouched.

Private.

"Look, if you're really that cold, you can go inside, or I can get you a jacket."

She looked at him, and then noticed she was hugging herself as if her life depended on it. "I'll tough it out," she said, laughing. "It's really not that bad."

He set down the tongs and closed the hood over the steaks, his eyes on her the whole time. "Are you sure?" he asked, the dip in his tone sending goose bumps up and down her arms.

"I wouldn't turn down some extra body heat," she said, "if you're offering."

Spencer moved closer to her. He placed his hands on her shoulders, and she held her breath. When he lowered his head, she tilted hers back. His lips brushed across her mouth as he put an arm around her and pulled her against him.

He smelled of soap, but also something mysterious and earthy. Just like his mountain. She rested a palm on his chest and splayed her fingers, wishing she could touch skin and the hint of dark hair at the vee of his shirt.

Just as the kiss was beginning to heat up, he lifted his head. "You never answered my question. Why didn't you want Dusty to know about tonight?"

"I don't care one way or the other. When he didn't bring it up, I figured you decided not to say anything to him." Her heart had picked up speed. Surely he could feel the hard pounding, though he couldn't know it was because she'd told him only part of the truth.

His arm tightened around her, and he claimed her mouth again. She kissed him back, welcoming his leisurely pace. Slow was good. For now. Because she didn't know what she wanted to do yet. About Spencer.

Or Jason.

Or about Moonlight Mountain.

War waged inside her. She wished he'd never brought her out here. Seeing the mountain as he saw it was making things difficult to sort out. From a filmmaker's standpoint, Moonlight Mountain was pure gold, and she yearned for it more than she'd ever wanted any other location.

But from the perspective of a woman—hell, a decent human being—she knew what might happen once Jason got a hold of that mountain. Oh, the crew would leave the property in perfect condition. She hadn't lied about that. But once the mountain was captured on film, there would always be tourists. Probably other interested directors. And Spencer's solitude and privacy would be gone forever. Could she really do that to him?

Damn her vivid imagination—great for crafting stories. Terrible for making sound decisions.

She slid her arms around his neck, and with her

breasts crushed against his chest, she could feel his heart beating just as wildly as hers.

His other arm came around her, and she felt the pressure of his hand at the small of her back. She buried her fingers in his hair, even as she warned herself to hold back. Just for now—give herself time to think. His hand moved lower to the curve of her backside. She felt the heat of his erection pressing into her belly.

It was no use.

Erin knew right then and there she was going to have sex with him. She'd have to be out of her damn mind to let the opportunity pass. He had nothing to do with the Hollywood crowd, and she could keep business separate.

He gently squeezed her backside. The tip of his tongue touched her bottom lip, and with a soft sigh, she parted her lips. Ignoring the invitation, his mouth moved to her jaw. He teased her with tiny slow kisses to her ear and back, before he slipped his tongue between her lips.

Lowering his other arm, he cupped her bottom with both hands, and she rocked her hips against him. He shuddered, the slight vibration in his chest making her breasts tingle in response.

Three quick beeps cut through her helpless whimper.

She hadn't imagined the sound because Spencer stiffened, as well.

They both pulled out of the kiss at the same time, and he muttered a mild curse. "It's my watch. I have to turn the damn steaks."

His vain attempt to shut off the timer ended with three more beeps before he made it stop. Erin understood his frustration all too well. But when he glared at the grill, she had to laugh.

He looked back at her. "What are we doing?"

Pretty loaded question. It sobered her instantly. "First, why don't you go ahead and turn the steaks?"

"Right." He walked the few steps it took to get to the barbecue and nearly ripped the top off.

When he fumbled with the tongs, she bit her lip. She had no business laughing. She could barely breathe, and her knees weren't all that steady. Yet he'd posed a good question. Now that she wasn't plastered all over him, she should really consider if this was the most irrational, foolish thing she'd ever—

She heard the hood close. The next second he hauled her into his arms until her body was flush with his. Erin pushed up on her toes, straining upward to meet his hot, demanding kiss.

10

SPENCER HAD NEVER met a woman who moaned so much from kissing. The soft, breathy sounds whispered up and down his spine and stroked his cock. Damn, it was hot. Finding that sensitive spot at the back of her neck, he brushed his lips over it. And got the response he wanted. Erin rubbed her breasts against his chest…just as she'd done before.

This teasing was killing him. They were both responsible for striking the match, and he usually enjoyed a slow burn.

But Christ…

He'd honestly thought he had more willpower than this. But her nipples were hard, and they'd been that way for a while. He'd tried to think of other things. Like the first big snow that could make his life a living hell. He thought about her movie buddies descending on the area and driving him nuts.

Nothing helped.

Not when he could smell the sweet warmth of her skin, the seductive scent of vanilla in her hair.

He swore he could smell her arousal. Imagined or not, it was about to bring him to his knees.

He wanted to see her. Touch her. The searing need was burning a hole in his gut.

She put her arms around his waist, slid her hands down to his ass and squeezed, just as he'd done to her. Spencer smiled and lifted his head. Her satiny skin glowed in the moonlight.

"I should warn you," she said, "if your watch beeps, I'm going to stomp on it."

He frowned. His watch?

"Ah, shit. I forgot to set it." He turned to the barbecue. "How long has it been?"

"Five minutes?" Erin shrugged. "An hour?"

They both laughed.

Without bothering to check the meat, he switched off the gas. "If they aren't done, we'll finish them inside."

"Later."

"Definitely later," he agreed and took in her flushed face, her eyes bright in the moonlight. He reached for her, but she evaded him and grabbed the platter.

"Come on. Hurry," she said, and then, "Wait," when he complied. She pointed to the tongs.

Right.

He'd no sooner transferred the steaks to the platter when she made a beeline for the door with it. She was either really cold or really horny. He hoped it was the latter.

He caught up with her in the kitchen. Erin set the platter down on the counter, turned around and pulled him into a kiss that made his spirits and just about everything else soar.

She clutched at his shoulders, kissing him for all she was worth, then changed direction and yanked his shirt from his jeans. Stopping just as abruptly, she asked, "When do you expect Dusty to come home?"

"Late. Maybe tomorrow."

"Awesome" She let out a small squeak when Spencer worked a hand under her sweater.

He skimmed his palm over her belly and up between her ribs. Her skin was just as smooth and soft as he'd imagined. The bra, though, he hadn't expected. He cupped the weight of her breast through the lace and silk teasing his palm. "Is my hand too cold?"

"No," she whispered. "Don't stop." Her lids drifted closed, and she swayed a little.

He backed her up to the closest flat surface. The instant her body was flush against the pantry door she became alert, excitement flashing in her dark eyes, her mouth curving slightly as she offered up her lips.

Spencer got the message. She wasn't looking for a slow, gentle wooing. He kissed her hard, thrusting his tongue into her sweet, welcoming mouth. She moved her hands up to his shoulders and then pushed her fingers into his hair.

His greater height and her flat shoes gave him about a seven-inch advantage. But she had no problem locking her fingers behind his neck and pulling him down to be right where she wanted him. And he had no problem with that.

Then Erin started doing it again. Making those soft, sexy moaning sounds that would likely end with him disgracing himself. After one particularly husky purr, he almost looked to see if she'd started without him.

Christ. This was crazy. He had a nice, comfortable king-size bed. Why were they standing in the damn kitchen?

Hoping to get her upstairs, he broke the kiss.

The woman moved quickly. Her hand had gone from his neck to the front of his shirt in a flash. The second she discovered they weren't buttons but snaps, she grinned, and with one good jerk, she pulled the shirt open. "Awesome."

Spencer chuckled.

"Sorry," she said, her smile turning mischievous. "My vocabulary tends to shrink at a time like this."

"Too bad. You have a great voice."

She laughed, the sound deep and throaty, and rasping all the way down his spine.

Damn, she was killing him.

His shirt had been pushed off one shoulder before he realized what she was doing. "Hey, guess what?"

She pressed her lips to his chest and glanced up at the same time she licked the skin between his pecs.

"I was going to say I have a bedroom," he murmured through clenched teeth. "But who gives a shit."

"Where?"

He felt his buckle loosen. Sucking in his belly, he looked down. "What?"

"Your bedroom?"

"Upstairs," he said and caught one busy little hand as she tried swatting him away.

"Too far."

Her earlier frenzy and this single-minded determination surprised the hell out of him. But goddamn, it was hot.

It took some effort, but he finally managed to capture her other hand before she could finish unbuckling him. He had her trapped. His body pinned her against the door. She tried an experimental wiggle but didn't struggle. And when she flexed her hips, a deliberate move that put pressure on his cock, he ground his teeth hard.

"Will you listen to me?" he said, shifting both her wrists to one hand.

She responded with more hip action. In self-defense and to remind her that he still had the advantage, he tightened his hold and jerked her arms up over her head. He wasn't rough but made it clear she wasn't going anywhere until he released her.

Erin didn't look shocked or upset. She just smiled.

Of course she liked it.

Spencer might've laughed if it wasn't so painful. "I'm going to let you go," he said, "and then we're going directly upstairs."

Erin nodded, her eyes dark with wicked intent.

"No funny business. Understand?"

Her husky laugh ended with a gasp when he rubbed her hard nipple through her sweater. She lowered her lashes, and he felt a shiver travel through her body.

"Promise me," he whispered, brushing the tangled hair away from her face.

Slowly she opened her eyes. "Let's go."

Damned if he wasn't having trouble pulling away. He liked the way she fit against him. He liked the scent of her skin, the smell of her hair. He liked the softness of her lips and the taste of her sweet, sweet mouth.

She was smart, confident and knew exactly what she wanted.

Erin Murphy really did it for him.

Why couldn't he have met her sooner? Back in Boise, when he'd still had something to offer a woman…

The confused expression forming in her eyes jerked him out of his odd stupor. He needed sex. Uncomplicated sex, and not any particular woman.

He wasn't worried. Erin was here and willing. It had been too long since he'd had female company. Once his physical needs were met, he'd be thinking more clearly.

His gaze dropped to her mouth. The urge to kiss her

was strong…until he saw her bottom lip quiver. The flicker of vulnerability in her eyes that quickly vanished. He'd seen it once before. He sure hated seeing it now. Maybe she was having second thoughts.

Releasing her wrists, he pulled away from her. "You okay with this?"

Erin frowned slightly, then grabbed the front of his open shirt and tugged him down for a quick kiss. "Definitely okay."

"Good," he said, motioning to the stairs.

She slipped around him and hurried across the kitchen. He straightened his shirt and grabbed a bottle of wine before following her, staying several paces behind to enjoy the view.

Halfway up the stairs she glanced back at him. "Oh, wine. Excellent. What about glasses?" she asked, turning around and skipping down two steps. "I'll get them."

He shook his head, not about to lose ground now. "Keep going."

"It'll only take a second," she said, descending another step, raking a gaze down his bare chest, her lips curling in a slow smile he knew meant trouble.

"Don't start anything," he warned, which she ignored by taking another step. "What if Dusty comes home early?"

She stopped, her eyes widening, then spun around and beat it all the way up to the second floor.

Spencer watched her turn left. "Last room on the right," he called out and indulged himself in a quiet chuckle when she changed direction without a word or a glance.

"Wow." Erin stood just inside his bedroom, staring at his bed, covered with a deep burgundy comforter. "Do you always make your bed?"

"Half and half." This morning he'd even changed the sheets—just in case. But he left that part out.

"This is nice. Almost bigger than my apartment. And Lila and I share it." She shrugged. "Of course, neither of us has been home much lately. Oh, and the fireplace. I'd forgotten."

He set the wine on the dresser and moved in close behind her, putting his hands on her shoulders, massaging gently.

She let her chin drop and swept her thick hair to one side, off the back of her neck.

Spencer smiled. "Subtle," he said, breathing her in and willing his cock to be patient.

"That's me." She sighed when he used his thumbs at the base of her scalp. "God, you have great hands," she murmured, trying to kill him with one of her signature moans. "I'm seriously going to want more of that later. But for now…" She turned to face him and ran a hand up his exposed chest, her palm smooth against his skin. "Enough small talk."

Nothing was going to stop her now. Determination gleamed in her eyes as she pushed his shirt off both shoulders, then she resumed the attack on his buckle. Her hands worked quickly, echoing her earlier fervor.

"Wait," he said calmly and hated to see her wince.

"Sorry." Shrugging, she dropped her hands to her side. "It's been a while."

"Yeah, for me, too."

She reared back, narrowing her eyes. "Really?"

"Yep."

"Well, hell, this is only gonna last two minutes."

Spencer laughed. "Bet you round three and four it doesn't."

"Game on."

Before she could get her hands on him, he pulled up her sweater. She blinked and raised her arms. Her lace bra was a shade darker than her pale, creamy skin. It seemed that smart, sensible Erin liked sexy lingerie. Spencer could appreciate that. He was a big fan, himself.

He tossed the sweater at the chair by the window before leaning in for a taste. He traced the valley between her breasts with his tongue, and she trembled against his mouth. She put a hand on his shoulder, and he let her steady herself while he unfastened the front hook of her bra.

The sight of her perfect rose-tipped breasts fueled his need for her. He rubbed a thumb over her hard nipple and watched as a shiver washed over her body. Her free hand curled into a small fist at her side. He felt her fingers dig lightly into his shoulder muscle.

Her lashes fluttered, and she seemed to be struggling to keep her eyes open. The flesh around her nipple was soft, so damn soft. He covered her high, round breasts with both hands, and she arched into his palms. Her tongue slipped out to dampen her lower lip.

Every cell in his body was on fire. He was damn close to rekindling her earlier frenzy. His hands itched to rip off her jeans and anything else that got in his way.

His lungs suddenly burned from lack of air. He breathed in deeply and forced himself to retreat. Taking his hands off her was the first step; he even moved back a foot. But he could still see her, and the fortitude it took for him to look away had deserted him.

A flush crept across Erin's cheeks as she widened her eyes and searched his face. She smiled when she realized he was getting out of his shirt.

"Need help?" She claimed the space he'd deliberately put between them, the jiggle of her breasts distracting him.

"Thanks, but I'd prefer keeping all buttons and zippers intact."

Erin laughed. More jiggling.

Damn.

"Besides, I want to win my bet," he said, unsnapping his jeans and nodding at hers. "How about you get out of those?"

She wrinkled her cute little nose. "Actually, the way we left it… I'm pretty sure we'll both win."

"Okay, smarty, I doubt this will come as a shock. I'm not all that interested in logic or your brain right now."

Apparently she found that a lot funnier than he did. But her laugh—Christ, he could listen to it all day. Assuming he didn't die from an unrelenting erection.

She did that shimmy thing as she shoved her jeans past her hips, then down to her thighs. Her tiny panties matched her lacy bra. He waited, torn between wanting her to peel them off now and wanting to do it himself.

"Come on, don't just stand there." She held on to her jeans and blocked his view.

He quickly stripped down to his boxer briefs and threw the jeans at his closet door.

"And?" She waved a hand for him to move along with the process.

"We need to do something about these serious control issues of yours." He waited for a reaction. Hell, he knew she hadn't heard him. She was too busy staring at his erection. "Erin?"

"What?" She met his eyes. "I'm not controlling. Is that what you said?"

He moved closer. "Call it whatever you want." With

quick reflexes, he yanked the jeans out of her hands and flung them across the room.

"Hey!" Her fierce glare held more than a hint of excitement. She backed up until the bed stopped her. "Wait," Erin said, putting up a hand. "Look, there's something I need to say. I should've said it before now. About the contract and this—us—tonight…"

"The contract?" Spencer stopped just as he was about to reach for her. "Is this a trick? You're willing to play that dirty?"

"No. Of course not."

He touched a beaded nipple, enjoying the texture of it between his thumb and forefinger. "Just how likely do you think it is I'd say no to anything at this point?"

"I'm not trying to— This has nothing to do with getting you to agree. Oh, God, this is a bad idea." She turned her shoulder to break contact, looked around and then crossed her arms over her breasts, inching toward her sweater hanging off the chair.

"Hold on." He gently took her arms and put them around his neck. "I was teasing. It was in poor taste, and I apologize." He slid his hands down her sides, tightened them around her waist and pulled her against him.

Looking nervous, she tilted her head back to keep him in her line of sight.

Spencer smiled. "You've had your fun. Now I'm going to have mine."

11

Erin felt his warm breath on her face. His fun? That could mean anything. She was a damn lunatic for trusting this man. She didn't know him. No one did. Except Dusty and Matt Gunderson, and Matt not so much. Spencer had never given off a vibe that he was into kinky stuff. But you never really knew about someone.

His mouth moved to her ear, and Erin had a second to wonder if she should have insisted on setting the record straight. Let him know this was purely personal and had nothing to do with business. But then his teeth caught her earlobe, applying a gentle pressure that spread heat through her body.

Screw it. Spencer was a smart man. He'd figure it out.

His arms tightened around her, and she pressed her aching breasts against his chest. His skin was hot, so hot she could almost feel her bones melting. Standing wouldn't be an option much longer.

"Erin?"

She drew back to look at him.

The desire smoldering in his eyes made her dizzy.

"I'll ask only once," he said in a whisper. "Are you sure?"

She held in a laugh. She wasn't sure about one blessed thing. "Absolutely."

He picked her up, laid her across his bed and stripped off her panties before she could say anything else. He followed her down, bracing himself on one arm as he kissed her long and hard and deep, dislodging her last foothold on sanity.

She slipped a hand between them and tugged at the waist of his boxers, but he slid down until he was out of reach and could look up at her breasts.

Not much ever embarrassed Erin. But the way he was studying them made her feel self-conscious. "I promise there won't be a test."

A faint smile curved his mouth, but his gaze remained steady. "They're perfect," he whispered and moved to take a nipple into his mouth.

He sucked hard enough to make her squirm, then flicked the tip of his tongue over the other breast. She moaned so loudly it was lucky Dusty wasn't in the house, or even in the barn. But that didn't persuade Spencer to stick with a sure thing.

No, he moved lower, caressing the skin between her ribs with his hands, his tongue, his lips. Then trailing his mouth down to her stomach and putting her on alert. He lingered around her belly button with long slow licks, the barest hint of stubble rasping against her increasingly sensitive flesh.

At his sudden move lower still, she arched up and clutched at his shoulders but couldn't reach him. "Wait. Your boxers. Please."

He kissed the top of her thigh before glancing up.

"My turn to call the shots, remember?" he said, his gaze holding hers captive, as he slid a hand between her legs.

Time slowed as her pulse quickened. His nostrils flared. A groan rumbled from his throat. He flexed his jaw.

She blushed at the way he stared at her, holding her gaze steady as he slowly brushed the backs of his fingers against her. But she couldn't force herself to look away.

Spencer did. Finally. He spread her thighs a hand's width apart and looked down to see what he'd uncovered. She didn't let him in easy. Some instinct made her resist, clench hard enough that he looked back at her face, concern furrowing his brow.

She wanted him. And she trusted him, or she wouldn't be lying across his bed. But she couldn't ignore the small kernel of fear that warned her not to go down this particular rabbit hole.

"Erin?"

But then again, she'd always had an oversize imagination. She lifted herself up and kissed him, using the opportunity to hook a thumb in his waistband. That was as far as she got.

Spencer caught her wrist. "What's the matter?" he said with a lazy smile. "Don't like someone else being in control?"

She smiled right back at him. "Ah, you really think you're in control? That's adorable," she said as she laid back against the pillow and parted her thighs without giving too much away.

His gaze zoomed in on what she was offering. "You're a hard woman, Erin Murphy."

"You're looking pretty hard yourself." She gasped at the feel of his mouth on the inside of her thigh.

He pressed a kiss to her tingling flesh, leaving a wet trail to the edge of her core. For a second all she could feel was his hot breath gliding along the slit of her sex. The next second his tongue slipped between her lips and stroked her clit. Pleasure shuddered through her.

Somehow she knew with that breach, the game had changed again. No matter how hard she trembled, no matter how hard her thighs instinctively tried to squeeze together, Spencer wouldn't let up. He used the same steady pressure, the same unhurried pace as he explored her with his lips and tongue.

With all the energy she could muster, she tried reaching for him, but it was no use. She was too weak. Her orgasm was building quickly, and she didn't think she could delay it.

His hand skimmed over her belly to cup her breast. He plucked at her nipples, his fingers toying with them as his tongue plunged inside her.

Erin gasped as she came.

The sudden force of the first wave nearly jolted her off the mattress. She whimpered and flung her head back against the pillow as the sensations continued to roll over her, through her, around her. She shook with each new wave, gripping the sheets as hard as she could so she wouldn't drown.

Her brain struggled to make sense of what was happening. This was something new. A door had opened, a spark ignited. It was unlike anything she'd felt before, and she'd had damn good sex. But this? It was weird and overwhelming but completely wonderful.

It took several moments to see through the haze. She blinked once, twice. Still bleary-eyed, she tried to focus on Spencer standing beside the bed. When had he—

He was naked.

Two more quick blinks and she could see everything. The size of his erection made her swallow. He smiled down at her. "Give me a second."

She started to protest when she saw him open a dresser drawer and pull out a condom. His ass was beyond perfect; defined by just the right amount of muscle.

Another aftershock stole her away for a moment, but then he was back at the bed. He leaned down and kissed her deeply. She could taste herself on his lips. "Here you go," he said, his voice hoarse.

When had he gotten a bottle of water? "Thanks." Unable to recognize her own breathy voice, she found herself dying of thirst, and holy crap, he'd even taken the cap off for her. She drank half of it all at once. Her mouth was still dry when she looked around for a place to set down the bottle.

Her gaze fastened on his beautiful burgundy comforter. She carefully held on to the bottle and scrambled off the bed.

Spencer dropped the packet on the nightstand, his expression alarmed. "What are you doing?"

"We should've pulled this down," she said, tugging at the heavy quilt.

"I thought you were going to run out on me."

"Oh, no, we're not finished yet."

"No, we aren't," he said with a wicked grin and yanked the comforter half off the bed.

Erin huffed out a breath. "I was trying to keep it from..." The words died when she saw the fierce intent in his eyes. Her gaze slid down to his cock, hard and thick, the crown slick with want. "You win." She set the bottle on the closer nightstand and climbed back onto the bed.

He didn't move, just watched her as she crawled

straight for him. As soon as she was close enough, she rose halfway up on her knees, slipping her hands around to his bare ass. Beneath her palms his skin was smooth and taut, his muscles tightening as she pulled him toward her mouth. She stroked the hard length of him with her tongue, before licking the crown.

Cupping her head with one hand, he stood with his eyes closed, his entire body tense. His fingers tangled with her hair. "You have to stop," he said, his voice a raw whisper. "I want to be inside you."

She loved the slight salty taste of him and hated giving in, even if only for now. But she also wanted him inside her. Wanted him badly. The pressure had already started building again, between her thighs, inside her chest. Right behind it was need, a need that bordered on desperation.

"Condom?"

He reached toward the nightstand. "I think we should get this on quickly," he said, his breathing ragged.

"I agree." Her fingers were clumsy from excitement, but she finally managed to tear open the packet.

She rolled the rubber down his cock while watching his jaw flex. And he watched her right back with hooded eyes, so dark now, she couldn't see his pupils. Rocked by a nervous zing of anticipation, she scooted back to give him room.

He crowded her anyway, his big strong body looming over her as he tasted the skin behind her ear. As he let her feel the weight of his arousal. In response she started to squeeze her thighs together, but he wouldn't allow it. He used his knee to part her legs wider, then settled between them.

He angled his hips and needed no further guidance. The tip of his erection nudged her opening. He lingered, rubbing her, before he slid in fast and deep. He partially withdrew and thrust a second time, and she gasped for her next breath.

They found their rhythm quickly. They pretty much had to. With all the foreplay, she was too close. So was Spencer. His body trembled. He had the same trouble breathing she did.

She bucked up to meet his next thrust, and everything around her tilted. She clung to Spencer and he went still. They let out simultaneous cries. Then he moved along with each of her spasms, rolling like thunder through her body, until she thought they would both die from exhaustion.

By the time he finally stopped moving, she'd fallen back like a rag doll. He kissed her long and hard and collapsed beside her.

HOURS LATER ERIN felt something jerk her awake. She knew where she was—Spencer's bedroom—but when had she dozed off?

"I'd apologize and tell you I didn't mean to wake you," Spencer murmured, his warm lips moving against the side of her neck, his arm heavy across her waist. "But I'd be lying."

She shifted to look at him and felt the heat of his arousal imprint itself into her tummy. "I would've called you on it."

His short rumbling laugh tickled her sensitized skin. "No doubt."

"Did you sleep?"

"Twenty minutes, maybe."

"Any idea how long I slept for?"

He kissed her lips. "About five hours."

"No way." She shot up on one elbow.

"I'm kidding." His large hand, with those long, talented fingers, flattened on her stomach, gently forcing her back down. "It just seemed that long."

Smiling, she snuggled closer. "Are we on round three or four?"

"You don't know?"

It was too dark to make out his features. But then she didn't have to see to know his insulted tone was a bluff. "Ah," she said smugly, rubbing her palm along his stubble-roughened jaw. "You don't know, either."

He moved his hand up to her breast and thumbed her nipple. "I suppose it depends on what a round consists of. Do we care?"

"Nope," she said and giggled for at least the third time tonight. Disgusting. She *never* giggled.

The only light in the room was coming from the master bath. It was a ridiculously large bathroom that hadn't been part of the original home, according to what Spencer had told her when they'd taken a much-needed breather. He'd had the wall to the second guest room knocked down so he could accommodate a whirlpool she swore had a million jets. The closet he'd added was bigger than her car.

She thought she heard a noise. Spencer didn't react, so she figured it was nothing. She was getting comfortable wrapped in his strong arms when something clicked. "What happens if Dusty comes home before I leave?" she asked. "Will that be a problem?"

"Only if he didn't get laid tonight."

"What does that have to do with anything?"

Spencer thought for a moment. "I'll tell you, but don't say anything to him, okay?"

"All right."

"He wanted to ask you out, and I basically told him he didn't have a shot in hell."

"Ask me out?" She stifled a laugh. "What is he… eighteen, nineteen?"

"Nineteen. I told him he was too young for you, but he assumed I was warning him off because I was interested."

Erin grinned at him.

"I wasn't at the time. We're talking about the day you showed up out of the blue."

"So the short skirt and heels are what did it? One look and you suddenly had to have me?"

He pulled her closer. "It was this smart mouth of yours that did me in," he said and tried to kiss her, but she was laughing. "And these perfect breasts." He swiped his tongue over her nipple.

"Okay, wait." Arousal slithered all the way down her spine. She shoved at his shoulder. "We know how this ends."

He lifted his head and said, "You haven't had a problem with it so far," before he drew the second nipple between his lips.

She allowed herself a small pleasant shiver, then pushed him away. "I'm serious. I shouldn't be here when Dusty comes home. I'd hate for him to have any bad feelings toward you—" She stretched to get a look at the digital clock, shocked to see it was 3:20. "I have to go."

"Why? Get some sleep first."

"Uh-uh."

"Why drive tired? You have any early appointments?"

"I'm meeting with Sadie at noon. She's the mayor of your town, in case you didn't know."

Spencer smiled. "I didn't, so thanks for the info." He rubbed a hand up and down her back and lightly kissed her shoulder, but something about his demeanor had changed.

Perhaps her mentioning Sadie reminded him of why Erin was in town. She would never bring up anything about the film or Moonlight Mountain at a time like this. Never. No matter what. But he had no way of knowing that.

She still thought she should leave soon, but not before they switched to a safer subject. "Are you and Dusty related?"

"No. Why do you ask?"

"Well, I know he's from Boise, and so are you."

Spencer's hand slowed. "I don't recall telling you that, so he must've said something."

So much for a safer topic. He resumed stroking her back, but she would have to have been made of stone not to feel the tension coming from his body. Not enough for her to get dressed and take off, but something had unsettled him.

She wished she could see his face better. "Actually, he's very protective of you. I couldn't get a word out of him."

"Why would you want to? You can always ask me what you want to know."

Somehow, Erin didn't believe that was true. Oh, of course she knew she could ask. But would she get a direct answer? "It's just that you like keeping to yourself. No one in town knows anything about you. So I figured—"

"You asked around about me?" He withdrew his hand, but he didn't sound *angry*, per se. A little annoyed perhaps.

"The first time I was here? Yes, I did. I was trying to find out who owned the mountain. A few people knew your name and when you'd moved here, but that was it. You were the mystery man who bought the old Baker ranch and named it Shadow Creek." She smiled and slid her hand behind his neck, hoping to relieve some of his tension. "Do you have any idea how many times I heard it put exactly like that? I expected them to pull out cue cards."

"Yeah, I don't like people poking their nose in my business. Just to be clear, I wasn't accusing you of anything."

She worked on the knot tightening the right side of his neck. "So, why did you leave Boise? Or is the subject taboo?"

Scrubbing a hand over his face, he just laughed.

"I thought about backing off, but you already know I'm curious and persistent."

"Yes. You're right." He pushed back against the headboard until he was sitting up and grabbed the bottle of water off the nightstand. First, he offered it to her, but when she shook her head, he tipped it to his lips.

Erin remained turned on her side, supporting her head with one hand and tucking the sheet around her breasts with the other. If he tried to sidestep her questions even once, she'd drop everything. Say something inane about the weather before she took off.

He recapped the bottle and shrugged. "I was born in Boise. My parents still live in the house where my sisters and I grew up. Both girls are married and live with their husbands and kids thirty minutes from my folks. I love them all. But I was sick of everyone telling me what to do with my life."

"Oh." She hadn't expected that explanation. "Are they all ranchers?"

"No." He found something about the question funny.

"My mom came from a ranching family, but she loves the city life."

"And telling you what to do…"

"She tries," he said with an easy laugh that helped Erin relax.

"When she visited, did she help you decorate the house?"

"Yeah, she did most of it. She loves that stuff. I appreciated her coming out here."

"Your sisters? Are they older?"

"One is, but Lauren doesn't harass me much. Koryn can be a pain in the ass. She's cofounder of a local children's charity and has three kids of her own. You'd think she'd be too busy to annoy the shit outta me, but you'd be wrong."

Erin chuckled. "I have one brother. He's a sales rep and always traveling. We talk maybe twice a year, and he can piss me off in ten seconds. Every time."

"Your parents?"

"They live in Santa Clarita, where I grew up, and they work in downtown LA. The commute is insane, but they've been doing it since before I was born." Erin shrugged. "They've always loved their work, so good for them. I was an independent kid." Spencer kept looking at her as if he expected her to say something more. Yeah, she didn't like being in the hot seat, either. Not that she had anything to hide. "We weren't a Norman Rockwell family. Now, my friend Lila, whom I've known since second grade, her family is so perfect it's a little scary. I used to spend most of my time over at her house, so I know firsthand it isn't an act."

Erin didn't know what prompted him to put his arms around her and pull her against his chest. It couldn't have anything to do with what she'd just told him. She wasn't complaining about her childhood, or anything else, for that matter.

"I hope I haven't given you a wrong impression," she said, tilting her head back to look at him. "Because I really like my life. Sure, I'm not directing movies at the moment, but I will be. Soon."

"I know. Failure isn't an option. I remember."

"Right. Good to know you listen well."

His mouth curved in a smile, and he touched her cheek, a featherlike stroke that shouldn't have started her heart pounding like mad.

The instant their lips met, they heard a door close downstairs.

Erin leaned back. "Oh, shit. He must've seen my car, right?"

"Don't worry about it. I planned on telling him later, anyway."

"Telling him what?"

Spencer's brows rose. He stared mutely at her, looking very much like he'd been caught with his pants down. Which, in a way… "Anything you want me to tell him," he said finally.

"I don't care what Dusty knows," Erin said, patting his gorgeous bare chest and holding in a sigh. "As long as it doesn't interfere with your relationship with him. But—" She sat up. "I am going to leave now."

"You don't have to—"

She rolled out of his reach and swung her legs off the other side of the bed. "Yeah, I really do. I'm not here on vacation."

He nodded, his expression verging on sulky. That made her grin. "Am I going to see you later?" he asked.

"I don't know." She scooped up her panties and jeans

and nodded toward the bathroom. “Are you going to let me use your Jacuzzi?”

“As long as I’m in there with you, absolutely.”

12

Walking into the Watering Hole seemed like the most normal thing Erin had done in days. She hadn't been there often, but it still managed to feel homey and safe. Probably because of Sadie, who'd so enthusiastically helped the people of Blackfoot Falls open their doors to filming. There were still a few who weren't pleased about the intrusion, but on the whole, it was a win-win situation.

Even though they'd pushed the meeting back to 4:00 and Erin was ten minutes early, Sadie, looking spritely in a plaid shirt and comfy jeans, waved her over to a table near the silent jukebox. There weren't many customers, only a few cowboys at the bar.

"What can I get you to drink?"

Erin hadn't even sat down yet. "Is there coffee, by chance?"

"Freshly brewed." Sadie looked over at the bar, and Nikki, whom Erin had met, came right over.

"Mind getting us coffees?" Sadie asked.

"You got it." Nikki turned to Erin. "I didn't have a chance to talk to you the other night. I'm looking forward to the filming. I've never seen a movie being made."

"It's mostly hurry up and wait," Erin said. "But it's also pretty fascinating. There are so many people involved in every shot. You should make a point of visiting the hair and makeup trailer. That's where you can hear the best gossip."

The adorable bartender laughed but went right off to get their drinks.

"She's married to Trace McAllister, right?"

Sadie nodded. "Yep. They're real good for each other. It's funny about Blackfoot Falls. A lot of people find love in this silly old town. Must be something in the water."

"Well, at least you know with our crowd, we won't be here long enough for that kind of thing. But don't be surprised if there are a few broken hearts when we're done."

"Speaking of…" Sadie opened up a folder. "I made copies of the leases I had drawn up for the new businesses since you were here last. Each one has a clause to honor the agreement you and I made before they signed on."

Erin nodded. "I spoke to Mallory over at the Full Moon Saloon. She was familiar with what we're doing, but we didn't discuss fees."

"Yeah. We've also got the Cake Whisperer Bakery, the new steak house and the motel. I've spoken to all of the owners, and no one has any objections to the fees you offered."

"They understand that they'll only get money if we use their establishments, right?" Erin nodded her thanks at Nikki, who set down two mugs.

"But there's a payment if you only shoot the facade, correct?"

"That's right. Very small, though. Nothing compared to the fees the big-time Hollywood studios can offer. But once our film is shown, I wouldn't be surprised if you draw more interest to the town. I'll meet each owner in person. Talk them through it."

"Good deal." As Sadie put a packet of artificial sugar in her coffee, she studied Erin. "You having any luck with the hermit on the mountain?"

Her cell rang before she could answer. Jason again. The last person she wanted to speak to. Lila had already told her his mood had improved somewhat, but he continued to be on a tear about Moonlight Mountain.

Erin turned her cell phone off and put it back in her pocket, returning her focus to Sadie's question. It wasn't surprising that Sadie, who heard everything that went on in her town, had been told about Erin and Spencer's brief visit to the Watering Hole, and no doubt about every other second Erin had spent with him. The gossip must have spread like wildfire.

But that wasn't a topic for a business meeting. "He does like his privacy," she said finally.

"Can't blame a man for that. Even if he's got one of the most beautiful views in the whole county. But then, you know all about that."

Erin nodded, hoping her stupid blush didn't give away too much. Behind her, the door squeaked open, and she heard Rachel Gunderson's voice. When she turned to see, Rachel was with one of her brothers—Jesse, maybe—and a dark-haired woman Erin didn't recognize.

"That's Jesse McAllister and his wife, Shea. Another match made here."

"I can't tell if you're trying to sign me up for a dating service, or if this is a new town brand."

Sadie sat all the way back on her chair. "Huh. That would make a hell of a brand, now, wouldn't it? But I don't think we have enough bachelor cowboys."

"With that brand? You'd be turning them away."

"I'll have to mull that over."

"While you're mulling, I don't know what kind of hours you keep here, but when the crew's in town, I'd suggest that you open on Sunday, unless it's against your beliefs. It's the only day the crew gets off, and they drink like they'll never taste booze again."

"Must make for some rough Monday mornings."

Erin smiled. "Oh, yeah."

"I've met some of your crew, and I've also been warned by Ben and Gunner. It's useful to have ex-movie people at our fingertips."

"That's right. I keep forgetting they've worked on plenty of shoots. I'm sure they've laid out the pros and cons for you."

Sadie chuckled. "They warned me to look out for the stuntmen," she said, and Erin laughed, too. "I have an idea what's going to come down. I look forward to it."

"We'll shake things up for a bit. I can already tell you'll be a fantastic extra, if not more."

"Me? Being in the actual picture? No, I don't want to be in front of the camera."

"I think you'd love it. And so will most of the folks who live here."

Rachel stood with Nikki at the bar and called out a greeting. Erin waved, wishing she had more time to stay and chat, but pushing the meeting back had put her behind schedule.

Jesse and Shea came toward the table, and after the

introductions, something clicked for Erin. "Shea? I know who you are. You're involved with that large animal sanctuary outside of town, right?"

Shea let out a long-suffering sigh. "Yes," she said, shaking her head, her brown hair sweeping her shoulders. Jesse laughed and she gave him a look. "Safe Haven is a wonderful place. We've helped a lot of animals. I don't regret being a part of it at all. But…"

This time Sadie let out a laugh she'd been trying to hold back. "Uh-oh. Here it comes. Thanks, Erin."

"Me?" Erin leaned back, out of the line of fire. "I have no idea what's going on."

"It was you, wasn't it?" Shea narrowed her eyes at Sadie. "Let's see if I remember correctly… 'Shea, how about serving as acting director until we find someone? We'll only need you for a month, two months, tops.'" Shea did a pretty good imitation of the older woman. Erin was impressed. Shea put a hand on her hip and glared. "How many years has it been, Sadie?"

"Well, now, I don't think it's been years," Sadie said. "Has it, Jesse?"

A grin tugging at his mouth, he slid an arm around his wife's shoulders. "But it's for such a good cause, honey."

Shea pretended she was still upset, but it was obvious she couldn't resist her husband's smooch on the lips.

Well, hell, how could she? Jesse and the other McAllister brother Erin had met were damn hot.

Almost as hot as Spencer.

Erin thought for a second.

Nah, not even close. Not that she was biased or anything. She glanced at her watch. She was supposed to meet him soon.

"Tell you what," she said, getting to her feet. "How

about I come by Safe Haven sometime? If I see anything that we can use in the film, you can make a few bucks for the sanctuary."

Shea's face lit up with a smile. "That would be great. Ask for me or Kathy. We've been sharing duties."

"Good. I'll call."

With business settled, it didn't take long to excuse herself, although Erin did stop to speak to Ben and his partner, Gunner, for a few minutes outside the hardware store about the stock they were providing. But then finally, she was back in her room at The Boarding House, sitting at the small table with a rash of location pictures splayed out in front of her. Most of them were on her tablet, but she always had a number of Polaroid backups.

Her gaze went unerringly to the stack of Moonlight Mountain photos. It truly was one of the most remarkable sights she'd seen, and she'd traveled a great deal. It was the way the mountain changed with the light, the weather, the angle, the moon. A director's dream.

If only…

She wiped her eyes, only then remembering she'd worn makeup to her meeting, but at this point she didn't care if she looked like a raccoon. Her insides were in an uproar, and not just because she hadn't slept more than a couple of hours.

Dammit. She'd never felt this conflicted in her entire life. If Spencer wasn't…well, Spencer, would she be her regular, pain-in-the-ass, never-give-up, take-no-prisoners self? The answer to that was as plain as day.

She wasn't going to manipulate him into letting them shoot on his land. She'd ask one more time, strictly out of obligation and for the record, but there was no doubt he was going to say no.

Putting those pictures aside, she checked out the Polaroids of the other two mountains. No, neither would be perfect, but they'd come very close.

Jason was just going to have to grow up and accept, for once in his life, that he wasn't going to get what he wanted. For now, her priority was a man's right to privacy. That she'd slept with that man had nothing to do with her decision. Nothing.

SPENCER TRANSFERRED THE last bale of hay to the stack in the corner of the stable, grunting with the considerable effort it took. He was either out of shape or too tired from last night to be doing all this manual labor. Grit and sweat stung his eyes. He pulled the bandanna he'd been using from his back pocket. It was past damp. He used his sleeve instead.

He looked over at Dusty, who'd just finished mucking the stalls. Earlier in the day, before Spencer had had a chance to say anything about Erin, Dusty mentioned something about seeing her car when he'd gotten home around three. That was it. He hadn't seemed upset, so Spencer figured everything had gone well with the bowling alley waitress from Kalispell.

"Erin might be coming over later," Spencer said casually. "You okay with that?"

Dusty shoved the damp hair off his forehead and frowned. "Sure. Why wouldn't I be?"

"I know you wanted to ask her out the other day. Last night wasn't planned. It kind of just happened, and I don't want any hard feelings between us."

"Hell, you were right. I'm too young for her. She looks at me like I'm her kid brother. Anyway, I'm glad you two clicked. You need a woman like her. Ain't natural for a man to be alone all the time."

Spencer watched him pick up the water jug and take

a swig, not sure what to think. Dusty wasn't naive. He had to know anything going on between him and Erin was temporary. Strictly physical. Spencer wasn't about to point that out. However they defined their relationship, it was no one's business but theirs. Besides, she'd be gone soon, and life would return to normal.

The idea held a lot less appeal than it should. Of course, he was tired and somewhat irritable from lack of sleep and working double time. If he wasn't so damn worried about the snow predicted to hit next week, he'd be sacked out right now. He still wasn't 100 percent sure about this ranching business. Summers spent at his grandparents' spread when he was a boy had been a lot more fun. Go figure.

"Yep," Dusty said, holding out the jug and fighting a grin. "You're getting a little long in the tooth there. Better get what you can, while you can, if you know what I mean."

Speechless, Spencer stared at the kid. Then he flipped him off.

Water spewed from Dusty's mouth, spraying the floor and some tack he'd hung over an old sawhorse. "Doc," he said, laughing and wiping his mouth with his arm. "I'm shocked."

"What did I say about calling me Doc? Now you have to clean the tack." He nodded at the mess Dusty had just made. Spencer wasn't touchy about his age. Hell, he was only thirty-three. He didn't have a clue as to where the defensiveness was coming from. And about calling him Doc? Dusty had had almost a year to break the habit. "I should make you muck out the stalls again tomorrow."

"Hey, wait." Dusty sobered real fast. "That's not fair. This is supposed to be a democracy."

"Few things in life are fair, kid. Get used to it." Spencer checked his watch, muttering under his breath, "Long in the tooth." He shook his head. "Shit."

Dusty snorted another laugh. "I wish you could've seen your face. You know *I* don't think you're old. And really, I'm glad you're hooking up with Erin. Bridgette said she didn't think her friend would go out with a guy old enough to be her dad."

He chuckled at that. "Want some free advice from the old guy?" He pulled off his work gloves just as he heard his phone beep and dug it out of his pocket. "You and the other wiz kids need to stay clear of any jobs requiring math."

Erin had responded to his text. She'd be over in an hour. His heart pounded like he was sixteen again. He realized he was smiling at his phone with Dusty watching. Ignoring him, Spencer headed out of the stable.

"Hey, where you going?"

"To take a shower."

He finally figured out what was eating at him. All day he'd been thinking about Erin. Hoping he'd see her tonight. And again the next day. And the day after that. Talking with Dusty reminded Spencer it would all end soon. Too soon. He wasn't ready to close the book on this little fling.

And damn it, he'd never wanted a woman more in his entire life.

ERIN PARKED NEAR the flagstones that led to the front door, slid out of her car and squinted up at the sky. The dark, stormy-looking rain clouds matched her mood. It seemed as if Jason was deliberately trying to piss her off. Acting like a damn prima donna…that wasn't like him. Even weirder was that Lila said Jason had been in a decent mood since yesterday.

It was more obvious than ever his beef with her was solely about Moonlight Mountain. But her hands were tied. And he'd refused to give the two alternatives any kind of consideration, so that was on him. At least it helped mitigate her guilt.

Fat lot of good that had done her when she'd tried to take a nap.

She felt a raindrop splatter on her nose, and she pulled up her hood. So far there'd been only a drizzle. Thank God the ground wasn't muddy.

"Hey, Erin."

At the sound of Dusty's voice, she turned from the walkway and looked toward the barn. He motioned for her to join him. There was no sign of Spencer. Oh, jeez. She hoped this wasn't going to be anything awkward.

"Hey," she said, hurrying into the barn two steps ahead of the rain. "What's going on?"

"Nothing but work. We're trying to beat the snow." He swept the hair out of his eyes and stared past her. "Is that hail?"

"I didn't think so." She glanced outside. "There's no snow in the forecast."

"I'm not sure how much fence we have to mend. Might take us a month."

"Shadow Creek seems like a lot of work for two people. Do you ever hire extra help?"

"I ask the boss about that every time we fall behind." Giving her a wry smile, he moved the saddle he'd been cleaning to a pony wall. "He might still be in the shower and wouldn't have heard the doorbell. You can go inside, though."

"Guess I shouldn't have come," Erin said, relieved

the conversation was so easy. "I didn't know you guys were behind schedule."

"It'll be dark soon, anyway." He seemed more interested in the weather than their conversation. "Damn, I'm driving to Kalispell again tonight. I hope the roads don't ice up."

"The ground is still warm."

"That's true." Dusty studied her. "Your boss still giving you trouble?"

The question caught her off guard. Then she remembered he'd overheard some of her conversation with Jason yesterday. "He's stressed and being a pain in the ass." She sighed. "Nothing I can't handle."

Dusty narrowed his eyes as if he didn't believe her. What was that about? "I'm glad for you and Spencer," he said and hopped on an ATV.

"Um, okay." Erin stepped back when he started the engine. He was glad for them? What did he think was going on? "Thanks. I guess."

"Not that you need my approval," he said, chuckling. "Anyway, you might want to keep clear of me for a few minutes. I'm just moving this quad closer to the barbed wire so I can load it."

Following his gaze to the big rolls of nasty-looking thorny wire sitting in the corner, she moved out of the way. "Wait—by yourself?"

"Yeah, I think I can do it."

"Got an extra pair of gloves for me?"

He backed the ATV right up to the wire. "You're not helping," he said. "You'll get hurt."

Erin rolled her eyes. "Where are the gloves?"

Dusty picked up a pair from the floor of the quad and tossed them to her. She caught them, earning a few surprised blinks.

"I've worked every kind of job on a movie set, except for director of photography. That includes being a grip."

"What does that mean?"

"It means I've lugged and carried and packed gear that weighs more than I do, so don't think I can't hold my own."

"Yes, ma'am." Grinning, he cut the engine. "All I have to do is get the wire spooled on the back here. It shouldn't take long. You just stand there in case."

"All right. But it looks pretty awkward from this angle."

"Don't worry about it. I've done this plenty of times."

It didn't take him long to line up the back with the first bundle. When she moved in closer, she realized the bundles weren't as large as she'd first thought, but they were still pretty hefty.

Dusty hopped off the quad. When he lifted the wire spool, she saw where he would thread it over a long rod.

"So you gonna be here while they're filming?"

"I won't be here for the whole shoot. Next week I have to go back to LA for an awards dinner. Then I'll head for—" Erin frowned. "Don't you think you should be concentrating on what you're doing with that wire?"

"Hey, don't sweat it. I got it covered." Dusty looked up, grinning. "So, then, what's next? You're coming back, right?"

She didn't like this. He was making her awfully nervous.

SPENCER'S STEP SLOWED when he heard Dusty ask the question.

Although he was more interested in Erin's answer, so he leaned against the barn door, just out of sight.

It probably didn't say much for his character that he

was listening in. He hadn't planned it. After his shower, he'd seen Erin's car and figured she was in the barn with Dusty.

"You'll be coming back, won't you?" Dusty repeated.

"Can't say for sure."

Spencer's mood plummeted. Bad enough he hadn't expected her to be leaving so soon. But she didn't know if she was coming back? Damn. That didn't leave them much time together. He walked into the barn trying for a smile, but he stopped cold when he saw Dusty.

That idiot kid was trying to load the barbed wire by himself, and Spencer could see right off the bat he didn't have the angle or the strength. He almost yelled for Dusty to drop the damn bundle, but he didn't want to scare the kid and cause an accident…

"Son of a bitch." The bundle slipped out of Dusty's hands.

Erin made a lunge for it.

"Erin, stay back." Spencer ran faster than he had in his life, but his legs were putty and the barbed wire fell too quickly for her to grab.

She cried out when the jagged end of the roll sliced through her jeans before falling to the ground.

He reached her seconds too late.

Blood oozed from the tear, quickly soaking the denim.

"Shit." She dropped to a crouch, extending the injured leg, her face awash with pain. "I'm so stupid," she said, looking up at Spencer, tears filling her eyes.

"I know it hurts, sweetheart," he said in a low soothing voice he'd learned years ago. But his bedside manner was rusty, and this was Erin. It about killed him to see her bleeding. And the gash, from what he could see, went deep. "Let's get you up."

Dusty was yelling something, but Spencer didn't hear

what it was because he had Erin in his arms, walking her over to the cleanest spot in the barn, a table they used to rest their drinks on.

Once she was sitting, he took off his shirt. She was shivering, and he meant to put the warm flannel around her shoulders, but he needed a look at the injury without all the blood in the way. "Get me clean towels," he told Dusty. "Now."

"What are you doing?" Sniffing, she tried to push him away. "Don't ruin your shirt."

"Please, Erin, don't fight me," he said calmly and used his shirt to staunch the wound. He caught sight of Dusty making a dash out of the barn. "From the outside dryer."

"Right. Yeah." The kid was ashen, save for the two bright red spots on his cheeks. But he turned on a dime, and a minute later he was there with an armful of clean rags.

"God, Erin, I'm really sorry," Dusty said and cursed under his breath.

"It wasn't your fault." Her voice shook. "It was mine. You asked me to stay back."

"Hey, stop it. None of that matters right now." Spencer didn't like the size of that gash. Erin couldn't seem to look away from it, even though the bleeding was relatively sluggish. He nudged her chin up until she met his eyes. "We just have to stop this bleeding, and then we'll get you to the doctor's office in town."

"I don't need a doctor."

He clenched his jaw. "This isn't a minor scrape. You need stitches. And a tetanus shot."

"I do not. I had a shot last year, and I'm sure if we just wrap it tightly, my leg will be fine."

"It won't. I can't even tell how deep the cut is until I get it clean."

She swallowed and stared down at the wound. "It didn't hit an artery."

"And you know this from when you got your medical license?"

"I've had worse. Besides, I don't have insurance."

"Who asked? I'm taking care of this, and half of it's coming out of Dusty's wages for being such an idiot."

"I'm real sorry, boss. I swear. I thought I could handle it."

"Well, that wasn't very bright, was it?"

"Hey," Erin said, indignant as hell. "I offered to help. I didn't do a very good job of it."

"Between the two of you, there wasn't one working brain cell? What was it about heavy bundles of barbed wire that made it look like a walk in the park?" Spencer regretted letting his anger get the better of him. Not so much anger, but fear for her. She wasn't taking this seriously enough.

"Damn it, Doc. I'm sorry. I truly am. I'll never do that again. Ever."

"Look," Erin said, "all I need is some superglue."

Spencer opened his mouth, but he couldn't even come up with a comment for that.

"I've used it before."

"I think superglue isn't very good for something like this," Dusty said, looking closer at the wound and cringing. "It's pretty long."

"Well, I'm not going to the doctor, and that's the end of the discussion." Erin shifted, wincing hard, scooting closer to the edge of the table.

Her hands were shaking visibly now, and she'd gone at least three shades paler in just a few minutes. If he had to guess, he'd say she probably had a pretty low pain tolerance, which just made everything more complicated.

"You're not getting down from there, if that's what you're thinking," Spencer told her. "And whether you like it or not, you're going to the—"

"You can stitch her up. Right here."

"Dusty."

"I know. But this is an emergency."

Erin winced as he changed towels, then hit him with one of her curious stares. "Wait—earlier, did he call you Doc?"

Spencer ignored her.

Dusty scratched his jaw and looked at his boots.

"Why did he call you that?" She wasn't about to let go of this. Spencer could see it in her face and hear it in her voice. "Dusty, why did—"

"I used to be a veterinarian. Which in no circumstances means I can stitch up your leg."

"You weren't just a vet, you used to be a surgeon. Right?"

Fuck. He was going to kill Dusty, but not until Erin's leg was taken care of. "I'm not a surgeon. I'll never be a surgeon again."

"Good thing I don't need one," Erin said. "But if you can sew…"

"Even if I was willing to do it, I'd leave you with a scar. One you'd have to live with for the rest of your life."

"Do you stitch up your animals when they get hurt?"

"Not the same thing," he said, wondering if she even realized her eyes had filled with tears.

"It is, though." Erin reached over, trying to hide her hiss of pain, and gripped his jaw, pulling his head up until he met her eye to eye. "I would deeply appreciate it if you would help me out with this. I swear, I won't come back later bitching about it." She crossed her heart. "Scout's honor."

"You're not going to let up, are you?"

She shook her head. "And I think, given that I'm an incredible wuss when it comes to things like this, that sooner is a whole lot better than later."

He let his chin drop to his chest. It wasn't so much her stubbornness but the fact that she'd come right out and admitted she was in pain, when she'd clearly have preferred to hide behind her tough-girl act. "Dusty. Go get my medical bag. The big one."

"And if you don't have any Novocain or anything—I'll take whiskey," Erin called out to Dusty, but he'd already made a beeline for the house.

"I've got a numbing agent. And I think I'll join you in that whiskey when we're finished."

"How come you're not a surgeon anymore?"

Spencer groaned, but he didn't have the wherewithal to argue with her. "First of all, I was a *veterinary* surgeon. I hurt my hand. I don't have full use of it, and sometimes I have a tremor. Which means I'm going to leave you with a scar."

"So you've said." She jerked at the pressure he applied, then drew in a ragged breath. "How did you get hurt? A car accident?"

Jesus. The questions were akin to torture. But knowing she was in pain, he couldn't tell her to shut up. "Why do I even like you?" he asked. "You make me crazy. And we haven't even known each other very long."

"You like me?" Her grin made him smile a little.

"Sometimes."

Erin laughed. "Ooh." She clutched his arm and bit down on her lip. "Remind me not to laugh, okay?"

"I know, sweetheart." He started to touch her hair, but his hand was covered with blood. Erin's blood. His hand shook.

Goddammit. Not now.

He could see the scar, and he remembered the day the accident happened as if it were yesterday. Except it hadn't really been an accident. Simply a result of his arrogance.

"You look cold," Erin said softly. "Is there something out here you can put on? I promise I won't move."

Spencer stared blankly at her. He glanced down at his bare chest, then back at Erin. She was in pain and concerned for him. And she was right. The chilly air was cold against his sweaty skin. Maybe that was why his hand was unsteady.

He could only hope…

Dusty returned, and it was clear from his hair and clothes that the rain was really coming down.

Spencer again switched towels on her leg, which, thankfully, was starting to coagulate. "Press this down as hard as you can. It's gonna hurt, but not for long, okay?"

"Yes, Doctor."

"And you can stop that right now." He glanced at the bag. "Are you allergic to any medications?"

"Not that I'm aware."

He turned to Dusty, who was so pale Spencer hoped he didn't pass out. "Get her some water and a pain med from the bag. Then stay with her while I go wash my hands."

Dusty hopped to it.

On his way to the sink, Spencer found an old sweatshirt in the supply closet. He put it on, pushed the sleeves as far up as they would go, then scrubbed his hands.

Luckily, Dusty was still standing. Spencer gave the kid a nod of thanks, mixed with an apology. He hadn't done anything on purpose. Spencer had just been so damn scared for Erin…

He couldn't allow the memory of watching her go down haunt him.

Pushing it aside, he got to work gathering everything he'd need, and by the time he'd sterilized the equipment as best he could, she wasn't feeling much at all in her thigh. Then he began a session that was just shy of outright torture. For both of them.

He'd taken such pride in his work, even something as simple as stitches. And now he was sweating like a first year.

ERIN'S LEG DIDN'T hurt quite so much. Mostly due to the numbing stuff Spencer had applied. The pill probably hadn't started working yet.

She'd begun by watching Spencer take the first stitch. Huge mistake. It was evidently fine with her stomach to get shots, even ones that hurt a lot, but sewing her skin together?

Nooo—followed by a million exclamation points.

Oh. Okay.

Maybe the pain med *had* made its way through her system.

Breathing in slowly, she kept her gaze on Spencer's gorgeous face. He was a study of focused energy, of patience and fortitude. But he was also sweating, and she could see how much it hurt him when he had to stop because of a tremor.

If only he'd taken her at her word that she didn't

care about a stupid scar on her thigh, this could have been a breeze. But no. When she'd argued that her legs weren't that great to begin with, he'd looked as if she'd insulted his honor.

Somehow, she had to get just a bit of that focus away from his sewing project—

Okay, not a good idea to call it that. "Dusty?"

"Yeah?" he said and stopped pacing like an expectant father as he'd been doing for the last twenty minutes.

"Do you know where Spencer keeps the good whiskey?"

Dusty laughed a little. "He only has good whiskey."

"Then how about you bring a bottle and a couple of glasses out here."

"I'll be right back."

"Hold on," Spencer said. "No alcohol with pain medication."

"What? The stuff you gave me? Pfff." She waved a hand. "I can hardly feel it."

Spencer briefly glanced up and gave a stern shake of his head.

She waited until he looked down again and motioned with her chin for Dusty to get moving.

True to his word, he started running immediately, which didn't give her the chance to ask him to bring some rain gear at the same time. Oh, well.

"Am I hurting you?" Spencer's voice was low, and odd.

She didn't like it. "No. I'm fine. Numb as can be. How about you?"

"Also fine."

"You going to tell me how you hurt your hand?"

"I'd rather not."

"But you like me."

He stayed focused on her leg. "Which means my humiliation will be worse."

"Oh, now you have to tell me."

He stopped. Looked up at her. "Really?"

"No," she said, seeing something stark in his eyes she wished she hadn't. "Actually, no. You don't. In fact, I'll never bring it up again. I'm sorry. I was teasing, and I don't ever want you to feel bad about telling me anything. Unless, you're like a serial killer or something, which, I admit, is a long shot, but I'd like to get a heads-up on that kind of thing."

He smiled, which was all she really needed from him. "So, you can hardly feel the painkiller, huh?"

"I'm not sure. Do they usually make people horny?"

Spencer froze completely. "Okay," he said with another stern look. "Enough. No more talking."

She noisily cleared her throat. "I can't help it. Sometimes silence bothers me. In a case like this, for instance." She paused and added, "Ow!" It didn't sound all that convincing.

"Jesus. You can be annoying."

"I know."

After a long awkward silence, she glanced up at the rafters, wondering if any birds lived up there in the summertime. She'd really meant it about not asking him again. Even though it was sooo hard not to.

"Rodeo," he muttered, then his focus switched to whatever he was doing by her thigh.

Damn she was going to miss these jeans. He'd whacked them off so high, she didn't dare cut the other leg and use them as shorts. "Wait." She blinked at him. "What did you say?"

"I was riding in a rodeo. I used to bareback ride for fun. Not even for money." He shrugged. "I was good at it. Some of my friends urged me to go pro. But it had always been just a hobby. Veterinary surgery was my passion. And I screwed up."

She waited for him to further explain. But he'd looked at the small scar on his wrist and clenched his jaw. She couldn't bring herself to ask him anything else.

"I was a damn good surgeon. Mostly large animals, but dogs and cats, as well. I made it through eight years of school in seven. Spent another year as an intern, three years residency after that and then ended up partnering with the guy who helped train me. Two months later people were wait-listed to see me. I was young to have such a good practice. Honestly, I had it all. A great job, plenty of challenges, a penthouse apartment—"

He wasn't finished, but he'd stopped, and she let it be. No wonder he was talking about all that stuff with Matt Gunderson. "Doc Stapley, the guy I partnered with, he might have just said it to be kind, but he used to call me the most gifted surgeon he'd ever met. He also called me a goddamn fool for risking everything. I didn't listen. I thought he was being overly cautious, worrying for nothing. My dad—he's a cardiologist—he told me the same thing." Spencer paused again. She thought he might've sewn another stitch, but she couldn't bear to look.

He turned to retrieve something from his bag. "The mare threw me, my hand got caught on the rigging handle. I broke my wrist, had to have tricky surgery to use my hand at all." He stared down at the scar. "I guess you could say I was lucky. Except the bubble had burst, and all because I was an arrogant idiot who thought he was infallible."

"We all make mistakes," she said softly. "But some cost more than others."

"Mine cost my life. As good as. I had to get out of Boise as quickly as I could. My family was in my face, colleagues, and the woman I'd been seeing, Kelly." He shook his head, sighing. "My love of animals hasn't dimmed. So I found this place. Now I'm learning to be a rancher. It's not as glamorous..."

"No?" She glanced around at the clumps of hay scattered everywhere. "You don't think so?"

"I'm not complaining. I'm serving my sentence quietly."

Erin's breath caught. She ached to think that was how he viewed his life now. As soon as she trusted her voice, she said, "Well, I'm very glad you're here, but I don't understand something."

His brows rose, resignation lurking in his eyes. He probably expected her next question. "Just one thing?"

"Basically, yeah. I get that you can't be a surgeon, but your hands work really well outside of that. Trust me. I know. So why aren't you still a vet? You have all that training, and plenty of animals still need vets."

"You make a fair point," he said slowly. "One I'm not willing to discuss." He looked up at her again. "We good with that?"

"Yep. Good as gold. Now, where is that boy with the whiskey?"

He choked out a laugh. "No whiskey. I mean it."

The moment he dropped his gaze to his work, she lost her smile. She really must be missing something big, because she didn't understand his reluctance to practice. It took a long time to become a veterinarian. More than it took most people to become doctors. She happened to know because her cousin was a vet, and he'd gone to school for a long time even without specialized surgical training.

A small ranching town this far north could use another vet. Even if Spencer only pitched in a few days a week, he'd do so much good. And not just for the animals he'd help.

Spencer needed to feel whole again.

And she thought she just might have the perfect idea.

13

SPENCER'S HAND ACHED SOME, but it felt better than expected. He was even pleased with the work he'd done on her leg. Not that he'd admit it.

Good as gold.

No damn way she was going to leave this alone. The woman never gave up. And if she started pushing him, they were going to have a problem. His hand was healing nicely, but inside he was still hurting and he didn't need reminders of his foolish arrogance.

Waiting for Dusty to open the back door, Spencer shifted Erin in his arms.

"As much as I'm enjoying this," she said, snuggling against his chest. "I feel duty-bound to admit that I can walk."

"You think so?"

Erin stiffened, before lifting her head to look at him, her eyes wide. "What do you mean? I can walk again, right?"

Spencer smiled. "Yes. Just not at the moment."

"Ha. Very funny."

"How's that painkiller working for you?" he asked, exchanging a grin with Dusty, who continued to hold the umbrella over Erin until Spencer carried her into the mudroom.

"Fine, I think. My leg is pretty numb." She let her head fall back to look at Dusty following behind them. "Thank you, Sir Galahad. Not a drop on me. How about you, Doc?"

He tried not to react. But they sure were going to have a talk later. "Nice and dry."

"Are you taking her up to your room?" Dusty asked.

Spencer nodded. "Go ahead and take off for Kalispell if you want," he said and saw the kid's hesitation. "Nothing more you can do here."

"Boss, I'm really sorry—"

"I know you are. And I regret biting your head off. It was an accident." Hell, if Spencer couldn't wrap his brain around that concept, there was no hope for him.

Dusty closed the umbrella and set it aside. Grabbing a rag, he wiped the trail left by Spencer's boots across the kitchen floor. Spencer had to smile. That was more cleaning than the kid had voluntarily done in a month.

"I mean it, Dusty. Get going while the rain has let up. She'll be asleep soon, anyway."

Her sigh ended in a soft purr as she rubbed her cheek against his chest. "I could get used to this."

Dusty let out a laugh and turned for the door.

Erin roused herself just as Spencer took the first two stairs. "I didn't mean I want to move in or anything like that. Just...you know, being carried around like I'm a queen or something."

"Can you be still so I don't drop you on the stairs?"

She nodded meekly. "Oh, wait. Is it your hand? Does it hurt?"

"Erin." He drew her name out, making it a warning.

"Okay." She snuggled back down against his chest. "But I have to say, this sweatshirt has seen better days."

Spencer groaned and laughed at the same time.

They made it to the bedroom without incident, and he dropped a clean towel on the comforter before he laid her on the bed.

He'd be glad to get her situated and comfortable, for her sake, of course, but also he needed to take another shower. Her jeans were a mess, what was left of them. The blood had dried, and miraculously her hoodie suffered very little spatter. While he'd cleaned her up as well as he could, she'd want to get out of those clothes.

After tucking a pillow behind her head, he brushed the hair off her face and straightened.

Erin blinked up at him. "Thank you," she said with a soft smile.

"How are you feeling?"

"Woozy."

Nodding, he said, "Probably a good thing you've never experimented with drugs."

"Who said I haven't?"

"Have you?"

"No," she said, backing it up with an indignant frown.

Spencer grinned. A full bottle of water sat on the nightstand. "Need anything before I get in the shower?"

"I can take one with you."

"No, you can't."

"But I'm all icky."

"We'll take care of that. Rest for now, and I'll find something that fits you."

"Okay." She nodded, her eyelids drooping. "Oh, how about your mom's robe?"

That completely stopped Spencer. He vividly recalled

giving the robe to Erin the day she'd slipped in the mud. Four days ago.

Four days?

That couldn't possibly be right.

"I'll buy her a new one," Erin said, somewhat defensive.

"No," he said, shaking his head, feeling as if he was in a daze right along with her. "It's not that—when did you come back to Blackfoot Falls? Was that four days ago?"

She wrinkled her nose. "I think so."

That didn't seem right. He counted back in his head.

Yep. Four days. How was it possible he'd known her for that short a period of time?

Erin was watching him. "It feels longer, doesn't it?"

"Yeah. It does." He bent down and kissed her gently on the lips. "And I'm not even on painkillers."

Laughing, she clutched the front of his sweatshirt. "I keep telling you. They're not affecting me." She pulled him toward her. "Has anyone ever told you," she whispered, brushing her lips across his, "you have an awesome bedside manner?"

"Thousands of women."

She snorted a laugh, covered her mouth and pushed him away.

Spencer laughed, too. It felt good. "I want you to stay right here and not move. I'll be in the shower for only a couple of minutes."

Erin sniffed the air and said, "Better make it longer."

"You're nothing but a wisecracking troublemaker," he said as he backed toward the bathroom. "You know that?"

"Yes," she said, grinning. "But you like me, anyway."

Shit.

He flexed his hand as he turned away.

Yeah, he did. Too much.

AFTER ERIN HAD washed up, she exchanged the robe for a long T-shirt Spencer had found, and seriously considered asking for another painkiller. Her leg burned like hell. More than she would've guessed.

But, no, she didn't like the effects of the pill he'd given her, so she'd tough it out if possible.

Using the light from the bedside lamp, she pulled back the gauze and studied the wound. Spencer had done an amazing job stitching her up. She'd bet anything it wouldn't leave much of a scar.

He entered the room carrying a tray, and when he saw what she was doing, he frowned. "You shouldn't be messing with that. Scoot back. I have some chicken noodle soup for you."

"What happened to the steaks from last night?"

"Dusty ate them when he got home."

"Both steaks?"

"He thought I'd left them out for him." Spencer motioned for her to move over.

"I'm gonna kill him," she muttered and slid back against the pillow.

"I'm surprised you have an appetite."

"I always do, even when I'm sick." She didn't really care so much about food at the moment. It was the principle of the thing. Damn Dusty. She ate chicken noodle all the time.

She watched him set the tray with the bowl of soup and the crackers on the mattress beside her. "Where's yours?"

"I'll get something. Let me wrap that back up."

"No, wait." She caught his hand and tugged until he

sat on the bed with her. “How long is that?” she asked, looking at her wound. “Would you say two inches?”

“Closer to three.”

“You did an amazing job. Can you not see that?” She saw his jaw tighten. “Okay, listen.” Shifting, she held in a whimper. “When you consider you haven’t been doing surgery and this was really sudden. You didn’t have time to prepare, or have the proper equipment or even a sterile place to work… Now, considering all that, don’t you think you did a remarkable job?”

“You’re right. The table wasn’t sterile. No telling what kind of infection you’ve contracted. I might still have to cut off your leg.”

She stared at him.

He smiled. “It turned out better than I expected,” he said slowly. “Is that what you want to hear?”

“I just want you to tell me the truth.”

“Ah.” He nodded solemnly. “Okay. Yes, I did a good job. You won’t have much of a scar. That’s the truth,” he said, his gaze level with hers. “Do you know how long it took me?”

Erin frowned.

“You were half out of it, so you probably don’t remember.”

She shook her head.

“Over an hour.” He flexed his hand, probably an unconscious reaction. But it chilled her to the bone, and she couldn’t stop a shudder. “It should’ve taken ten minutes.”

Erin wanted to cry. It hadn’t occurred to her how much it had taxed him physically… “Your hand hurts because of me,” she whispered.

“That’s not my point.” He cradled her cheek in his

palm. "Come on, don't be upset. I'm fine. But I can't take so long doing something as simple as—"

The first tears started to fall.

Pulling back, he frowned at his palm. He looked at her and wiped a tear with his thumb. "Erin, please. That's not what I was saying. I'd do it all over again even if it took five hours."

She really started crying then. She was a stupid, selfish moron. He gently pulled her against his chest. and she sobbed all over his clean shirt. "I'm sorry, I'm so sorry," she whispered.

"Shh. Stop crying," he urged in a calm voice. "You're going to end up hurting yourself. You need to rest."

Actually, she did hurt from him holding her too tight.

A round of hiccups didn't help.

She pulled away. What she saw chilled her. His voice may have been composed, but his face was a wreck.

"I'm fine, Erin. I promise."

She swiped at her damp cheeks. "Take me back to town, okay? Or maybe I'm all right to drive." She moved her butt a few inches toward the edge and winced inside. "I haven't had another pill, so I should be fine—"

He gently took her shoulders. "No."

She sniffled. "To which part?"

"All of it." He brushed her hair back. "I have no idea why you think that you suddenly need to leave, but I'm not letting you go anywhere."

"Well, you can't just keep me here against my will."

"Yeah, I can."

"That's called kidnapping."

He bit back a laugh.

"I'm serious." She used the neckline of his borrowed T-shirt to wipe her nose.

"Fine. When I take you to town tomorrow, I'll drop you off at the sheriff's office. You can file a report."

She tried to glare, but her leg burned like it was on fire and all she did was whimper. "Sorry," she murmured and turned away.

"Look, I want you to eat something. And then, if you need it, I'll give you a milder painkiller." He cut off her objection with a silencing hand. "It won't affect you as much with food in your stomach."

She stared stubbornly at the wall.

"Please," he said. "I did what you asked. Can't you return the favor?"

All the air seemed to vanish from her lungs. "That's not fair."

"Probably not." He picked up the bowl and dipped a spoon into the soup.

She used his shirt again, this time to dry her eyes. "You're not going to hand-feed me."

"That depends on you," he said, his face full of concern. And maybe there was some affection in his smile.

She scowled back. "Just because you're so damn hot doesn't mean you get to tell me what to do."

"No," he agreed, keeping a straight face and dipping the spoon in again. "Just for today, and only today, I'm your doctor. That's why you're going to do exactly what I tell you to do."

14

ERIN FINISHED HALF the bowl of homemade chicken noodle, making sure Spencer ate a sandwich and the other half of the soup. It was really good. She was surprised he'd made it himself.

When he handed her the water, she took it. When he held out the pain pill, she folded her arms across her chest. As far as she was concerned, they hadn't finished their discussion about whether or not she could drive herself to town. The last thing she wanted was to be a burden.

"I have certain conditions."

"Of course you do," he said, passing a hand over his weary face. "Does everything have to be a negotiation with you?"

"Yes."

"Okay." He moved the tray and sat beside her.

The next thing she knew he was kissing her. Carefully. Using his tongue and teeth to nibble at her bottom lip. One hand cupped the back of her neck as he explored her mouth before forging a path to her ear.

She had no idea how the pill ended up in her palm or why he was handing her the water again. But the second he broke away, he lifted her hand to her mouth, and before she knew it, she'd taken a sip and swallowed the tablet.

"That's how I negotiate." He took the water out of her hand and set the bottle on the nightstand. "Now listen, this medication is little more than an aspirin. But in case it makes you sleepy, are there any calls you need to make? Or if you need to check for texts…"

She hadn't even closed her mouth yet. "You did not just do that."

"Do what?"

Erin sighed. "So, if I knock out, are you going to take advantage of me?"

"Probably."

"See, this sucks. I want to be awake for that."

Spencer laughed.

"Okay," she said, patting the other side of the mattress. "More negotiating would be good."

He walked around the foot of the bed and started to settle on top of the comforter.

"Uh-uh. Stop right there. Take your shirt off and get under the covers with me."

"Look, kissing is all right, but we can't get crazy."

"Oh, you think I don't know that? Off."

He unbuttoned the shirt. "I should've given you something to knock you out."

"That wouldn't have been nice."

She crooked a finger.

"I'm getting there," he said, tossing the shirt aside and sliding in between the sheets, his movements slow and careful. "Just lie back. Can you do that for me without arguing?"

"Yes," she answered sweetly when he caught her earlobe between his teeth, gently, the slight pressure feeling oddly soothing. The sudden heaviness of her eyelids had her lashes drifting down, and she didn't even try to fight it.

"That's right. Close your eyes," he whispered in her ear and kissed the side of her neck. "And don't move."

She liked the warm feel of his body next to her. And where his chest brushed the side of her breast. Where his hardening cock pressed against her hip. Where his breath caressed her ear.

And yet, it wasn't enough. She wanted him closer. Bare skin to bare skin. His heart beating against hers.

She had to remember not to move her leg too much. Not just because it hurt. If she reacted to the throbbing, Spencer would stop. He'd leave her alone in his bed, and she would hate that so much more than any discomfort she felt.

"You should've taken off your jeans," she whispered.

"Later." He slid down and kissed her breast through the T-shirt while he slipped a hand underneath and covered her other breast with his palm.

Her nipples hardened beneath his touch, and he sucked on the one against his mouth, the barrier of the T-shirt somehow making it feel all the more erotic. His thumb brushed across her other nipple, making her moan.

His mouth moved back to her ear. "Tell me if I hurt you."

"That wasn't that kind of moan," she murmured.

"I know." He put his lips on hers and kissed her gently before pushing his tongue into her mouth, tangling with hers, stroking and teasing, until the hunger and heat started to build.

She shivered when his hand slid between her legs. It

wasn't easy remaining still when his fingertips teased the lips of her sex. But if she moved too much, he'd stop.

"Spread your thighs a little more," he said, and she obeyed.

"That's right. Perfect." His erection pulsed against her hip. He slid his fingers over her clit.

Erin jerked with an unexpected spasm. "Don't you dare stop," she said, clutching at his hair.

He drew her shirt up and sucked a nipple into his mouth. Hard. Harder than he had before. And she found she liked it. A lot. Urging him on, she dug her fingers into his muscled arm and arched her back just a little. After giving the other breast equal attention, he kissed the skin over her ribs.

Cool air skimmed her bare, damp breasts. He tugged the covers down to her knees as his warm lips continued to taste and tease. He rubbed his hard cock against her leg. But the denim was in the way, and she craved the heat of his smooth, taut skin.

"Your jeans—"

"Shh." He surged up and kissed her on the mouth, full and deep, before moving back down and claiming the spot between her spread legs.

First, he knelt, gliding his palm along the outside of her thigh, trying to distract her while he stole a look at her injury. It was fine, the bandage dry. She could've told him that. Pleasure had replaced pain after the first kiss.

But if he wanted to play the distraction game…

She caressed her left breast and toyed with her nipple, immediately capturing his attention. "I considered getting it pierced. What do you think?"

He smiled and lowered his head. His tongue parted her nether lips, and she bucked up in response.

"Easy," he murmured, his hot breath stroking her intimately, as sure as his tongue and fingers had.

Reaching up, he claimed the nipple she'd released. He tugged gently at the tight bud while the tip of his tongue circled her clit, increasing the pressure just as he slid his fingers inside her.

Trembling, unable to breathe, Erin clutched uselessly at the sheets. And then her body started to convulse, over and over, each wave of pleasure robbing her of more breath. Zapping her strength. Leaving her in a bleary haze. The house could suddenly go up in flames, and she wouldn't be able to move.

He did, though, to the side of the bed, and when she was finally able, she lifted her head.

"Is that it?" she asked. "Is that all you've got?"

With a faint smile, Spencer held her gaze, shucked his jeans and rolled on a condom. He got back on the bed and leaned over her. "What do you want, Erin?" he asked and found a tender spot between her breasts.

"You."

"More specific." He licked her belly.

"Inside me."

"Like this?" he murmured, caressing her inner thigh before slipping a finger between her lips.

"Yes." She tried to control her response, but the featherlike touch was driving her crazy. "No."

"You're so wet." His voice was low, mesmerizing as he slid his finger in deeper.

Letting out a startled gasp, she clenched. "More," she said. "I want more."

He whispered something she didn't understand. His breathing was no longer even. His hazel eyes were almost black. His hand, the one with the scar, resting on her belly, trembled slightly.

She shifted just enough to capture it, and she traced the scar with her lips.

"I want to feel you come inside me," she said in that low husky voice she knew he liked.

Spencer watched her suck his index finger into her mouth.

With a muffled groan, he pulled back his hand, grabbed a pillow and knelt between her thighs. He tucked the pillow underneath her butt. She could feel the head of his cock brush against her, teasing her, and she bucked up to receive him.

When he shifted away, she clutched at his arms and tried to pull him back to her.

He kissed her mouth and whispered, "Easy," into her ear…

At the same moment he entered her.

Slowly, only a few inches. "Jesus, you're wet," he murmured, his body shuddering, straining as he tried to hold himself back.

That's not what she wanted. "Please, Spencer," she said urgently when she felt him start to withdraw. "Don't. I want all of you."

He stared into her eyes and then pushed in just a little more.

"Dammit, Spencer."

He thrust in deep, filling her completely, and she swallowed a gasp. Her vision blurred. For several long, panicked seconds she couldn't drag in any air. She heard him moan and rocked up against him.

His eyes bore into hers before a hint of concern parted his lips.

"I'm fine," she said and clung to his arm when she felt him shift slightly. "Better than fine."

With a muttered curse, he thrust hard, drove deeper

into her. The sensation was as thrilling as it was scary. She didn't think he could stretch her any further. She tightened her muscles around his cock and squeezed. A tortured sound rose from his throat.

She refused to let go of his arm. She wanted him to act, not think. Granting her silent wish, he braced himself on one arm and started to move inside her. As if he wanted to be sure he'd touched every inch of her, mark her as his. Only his.

And for the first time in her life, Erin didn't think she would mind. Even as she prayed this would last all night, she began to unravel. The pressure was already almost at the melting point.

Spencer caught her hand. Startled, she looked at his face. He kissed her fingers, smiled, then dropped her hand and thrust so deep they both moaned. She arched once, then fell back as the convulsions overtook her. Spencer, caught up in his own orgasm, seemed to be straining to keep his weight off her as she shattered into a million sparkling pieces.

MORNING DAWNED UNDER a dreary gray sky that kept Spencer's bedroom dark and cozy. Despite how late they'd slept, Erin had snuggled deeper into the warmth of the thick quilt beside Spencer. Only when she'd heard him close the bathroom door did she realize she'd dozed off again.

Grateful for the privacy to whimper and cuss, she swung her legs off the bed and planted both feet on the floor. She barely felt anything. The skin around the bandage was bruised, but it wasn't as though she'd be wearing shorts anytime soon.

Erin found her phone on the dresser loaded with texts

and voice mails. After replying to Lila, she scrolled through the dozen or so messages that Jason had left.

Spencer walked out of the bathroom just as she muttered a curse. "That bad, huh?"

"You're wearing a robe."

"And you're not," he said with that wicked grin she loved. Coming up behind her, he wrapped her in his arms and kissed her shoulder. "How's the leg?"

"Good as new."

"Did you take anything?"

"Nope."

He cupped her breast and brushed his lips along the side of her neck. "You want pancakes?"

Erin wiggled against his erection. "You sure it's food you want?"

"Now that you mention it…"

Her phone rang. She'd forgotten it was in her hand.

"Need to get that?" Spencer asked, releasing her and stepping back.

She shook her head. Knowing he'd probably seen the caller ID from over her shoulder, she shrugged and said, "It's just Jason."

"I was going downstairs to make coffee, anyway. So…" Spencer returned the shrug, his eyes suddenly troubled. "Take whatever time you need."

"And pancakes?"

He stared blankly at her, his expression distant. She didn't understand why his mood had shifted. Jason's call shouldn't have triggered anything. Unless it had reminded Spencer of Moonlight Mountain and her mission to wear him down. He didn't have to worry about it anymore, but he didn't know that.

"I mean, since you'll be waiting for the coffee to brew…"

Spencer smiled easily. "Pancakes it is," he said, running his gaze down her body, lingering on her breasts and then her legs. "A kiss will get you a side of bacon."

Erin laughed. "Silly man. You could've gotten smooched for nothing." She tossed the phone back on the dresser and stepped into his waiting arms.

His hands stroked her back, and she rubbed her hardened nipples against his chest.

"I have something to tell you," he said, and she tilted her head back to look up at him. Desire burned hot in his eyes. "Before the day gets away from us."

Erin nearly melted into a puddle. She didn't dare read too much into that sexy, intense look.

Just lust, that's all.

"I'm going to sign the agreement. You can use Moonlight Mountain."

Wow, that was the last thing she'd expected him to say. "No." She shook her head. "No. You don't have to—"

"I know I don't. I want to."

"Look, Spencer, it's not that I don't appreciate it, because I know what an amazing sacrifice it would be for you. But honestly, I've reconsidered."

He studied her for a moment. "Sex has nothing to do with it. That's not why I'm offering."

"See, that's the thing. We can't know that for certain." She shrugged and stepped back, forcing him to release her. "But that's not the reason I won't let you do it. In fact, I'd decided against it before we had sex."

"Okay," he drawled, clearly puzzled. "Why did you change your mind?"

Erin opened her mouth, suddenly realizing she might want to soft-pedal a bit. The whole truth could make her sound pretty awful. She hadn't lied about the crew leaving the land in perfect shape, but she'd omitted the part about the mountain attracting attention.

"Your privacy is important to you," she said, "and I won't be responsible for compromising it."

Spencer caught her hand and tugged her back into his arms. "That's not the only thing important to me, Erin. So how about you let me worry about it?" he said and kissed her.

15

ERIN RETURNED TO The Boarding House just after noon. She dropped her room key on the bed, and next to it she laid the smudged white envelope. Inside was the lease agreement granting Crazy Coyote Productions access to Moonlight Mountain—signed by Spencer not more than an hour ago. Even after she'd told him not to sign it—no, *begged* him not to. Pleaded with him to give the matter more thought.

But he hadn't listened to a word she said. He'd scrawled his signature across the bottom, handed it to her and sealed the deal with a kiss. A damn hot kiss that hadn't allowed for more rational thought.

Well, that was the excuse she was using so she wouldn't feel like shit. The mountain was perfect—beyond perfect. And she knew in her heart that it was going to stir up some interest. So why hadn't she better explained that to Spencer?

Or why wasn't she jumping up and down with glee and calling Lila and Jason or anyone else who'd be impressed that she'd done it again, pulled a win out of thin air?

Instead, she just stood there, staring at the envelope,

certain she'd never felt more conflicted in her entire life. A shot at realizing her dream was almost within her grasp. Landing an assistant director's slot was huge. Not something a sane person could ignore. And she herself would love to use that mountain in the sequel.

Giving herself a mental shake, she switched her attention to the bag of first-aid supplies she was clutching. Before she'd left Shadow Creek, Spencer had checked her leg. The gash looked good, all things considered, and he'd seemed confident infection had been avoided. But he'd loaded up a bag with gauze, tape, ointment, and had given her strict instructions on how to care for the injury. All that despite the fact they were going to see each other later and there was no way in hell he wouldn't want another look at it then.

All the way back to town Erin had thought about the expression of surprise and wonder on Spencer's face as he'd inspected her leg. Oh, his concern for her was real, and he'd been pleased to see she was on the mend. But something so much more important had happened…he had seen for himself that hope wasn't lost. He could still use his hand. Even if only for uncomplicated surgery.

Erin was no expert, she knew that, but she could see the long row of tiny stitches was amazing work. She'd barely have a scar. Had she gone to the GP in town, she doubted he would've done any better. If anything, he probably would've used half the number of stitches, almost guaranteeing she'd be left with a noticeable scar.

Spencer still needed time to digest what the discovery could mean for his career. Completely understandable, even for someone as impatient as her. But a small push in the right direction couldn't hurt.

The first thing she had to do was to get out of his old

sweatpants. Even with the waistband rolled over twice, she had to keep hiking it up so she wouldn't trip.

But as she slid the soft, worn fabric down her hips, she thought about how wonderful Spencer had been to her, and, silly as it seemed, she wasn't ready to part with the sweatpants. Wouldn't hurt to wear them while she made her calls. She pulled them back up, all the way to her ribs. And the jacket he'd loaned her, well, she probably wouldn't ever take that off.

She turned her face to the collar and inhaled deeply. Of course his rugged, manly scent threw her pulse into overdrive. There was something else, though, something much deeper than sex.

Spencer made her feel safe. Content. Comfortable. Odd, because she'd never looked for any of those things in a man. This was totally new territory for her. She'd depended on herself for so long—from the time she was twelve and left to her own devices after school. Her brother had just joined the army, and her parents had never been around much. She knew they loved her, but they were busy with their careers. She got that.

Speaking of which… Erin picked up her phone and gave in to the inevitable. For once she hoped Jason answered. No more texts or phone tag. They needed to clear up a few things.

She got her wish. "Jason?"

"Yep. You caught me at a good time."

"Wow, I didn't think there was such a thing anymore."

"Only if I use the term loosely. We had a camera go on the fritz, so we broke for lunch while Kevin figures out what's wrong with it."

Weird. Erin would've expected Jason to be in a shitty

mood. Not just about the camera, but about everything… "You get a chance to look at those pictures I sent?"

"Hold on." His voice was muffled, and she could tell he'd lowered the phone and was talking to someone else. "Okay…" He was back. "What did you— Oh, the shots of the new storefronts. The bar and steak house should work great. We gotta do something about the bakery."

"Yeah, I already warned the owner." Okay, this was just getting stranger by the second. Why hadn't he mentioned Moonlight Mountain? If he didn't bring it up, she sure as hell wouldn't. "How's the schedule? You still making the move to Kalispell this week?"

"That's the plan." Jason hesitated. "It's one of the reasons I wanted to talk to you."

She had a feeling she should sit down and sank to the edge of the bed. Any number of things could've gone wrong, which he needed her to fix. Just part of the business. She hoped he wouldn't ask her to leave Blackfoot Falls *now*.

"And what's that?" she asked after a stretch of unnerving silence.

"The crew will pack up tomorrow evening and then head over to Kalispell the next day. I figured I'd swing by Blackfoot Falls before I met them there."

"Why?"

"So we can talk."

"We're talking now."

"I want to see the town," he said. "You know, get a feel for it before we shoot the last few scenes."

"Bullshit. Blackfoot Falls isn't even on the way." Erin didn't like this, not one bit. "What's the real reason?"

"So cynical," he said with a phony laugh.

"Is this about Moonlight Mountain?"

"Did you get it?"

It was her turn to hesitate. "I might be close," she said, feeling edgy and cornered. Something was up. Jason sounded distracted and a little bit nervous, and it wasn't at all like him to keep her out of the loop.

"Maybe I should talk to the guy when I get there."

Erin chuckled at that. "Hunt would throw you off his property before you got a word out."

"Yet you think you can turn him? You must have some hidden talents I don't know about."

This was the second time she'd sensed he was trying to piss her off. "More than you could ever dream of," she said, knowing her response would surprise him.

"Hey, I've gotta go. They need me on the set…"

"Jason, wait. What is it that you wanted to talk to me about?"

"I'll text you before I get to Blackfoot Falls."

"Don't hang up—"

The asshole had already disconnected.

She let out a frustrated shriek that was bound to bring someone to her door. Let 'em knock. Whatever the reason Jason needed a face-to-face, Erin didn't have time to worry about it. Her days in Blackfoot Falls were numbered, and she had a lot to do. She'd come back after the awards dinner, but once they started shooting, she'd be crazy busy. Of course, she'd still have time for Spencer. Every night, if it was up to her.

Oh, God. She couldn't even think about him without grinning like a twit. And that glimmer of satisfaction in his eyes after he'd stitched her up…she couldn't shake the image. He thought walking away from his other life would take care of everything. And maybe he'd end up happy ranching, but he had other options to explore. What kind of friend would she be if she didn't help him see that?

Enough daydreaming. She had work to do. Starting with a phone call to Shea McAllister at Safe Haven Animal Sanctuary.

ERIN STEPPED OUT of the bathroom and saw Spencer standing at the window, looking out toward the Rockies, their peaks shrouded in morning fog. With his back to her, only a towel wrapped around his narrow hips, the sight of him made her breath catch. She had to stop right there. Take the opportunity to look her fill.

His hair was slicked back, still damp from the shower they'd taken together. Just the right amount of lean muscle defined his shoulders and back, and she knew exactly what that towel was hiding. The man had a world-class butt. Being in the movie business, she'd seen plenty of naked asses and considered herself something of an expert.

He glanced back at her. "Do I pass inspection?"

Erin bit off a guilty smile. "Don't know yet. Give me another five minutes."

"Yeah," he said, turning away from the window. "That's not gonna happen." His mouth curved as he approached while taking his own leisurely appraisal of her, reminding her that she herself wore nothing but a smile.

She watched the front of his towel move. "Guess I passed."

Laughing, he caught her hand and pulled her into his arms. He kissed the tip of her nose, then brushed his lips across her mouth before leaning back to look at her. "It's still raining," he said with a slight lift of a brow.

Erin knew exactly where this was going. She helped things along with a subtle hip thrust and felt his body tense. "Raining or drizzling?"

"Doesn't matter." His hands slid down her back, and he squeezed her butt. "The ground's going to be muddy."

"Ah." She smiled, doubting the other ranchers would be using the excuse to take the day off. "I'm assuming you'll have some extra time on your hands?"

"That would be correct." He smiled when she gave his towel a firm tug, and it dropped to the floor. His growing erection pulsed hot against her belly.

"I'm sorry. I know that puts you further behind."

He half shrugged, his darkened gaze drifting to her mouth. His body heat surged with an energy all its own, caressing her breasts, penetrating her sensitized skin. It was hard not to give in to it. Let him take her back to bed. But Jason was coming tomorrow, and she had too much to accomplish before then.

"I know what would make you feel better," she said, rubbing her palm over his flat nipple, then letting her fingers trail down to his cock.

"I bet you do."

"A picnic lunch."

He blinked and met her eyes. "A what?"

"Don't worry, I'm not cooking or anything. I'll pick up something at the diner. Get Marge to pack something special for us."

Spencer didn't move or speak for several long seconds. Then he leaned back, frowning. "You aren't kidding, are you?"

Erin shook her head. "I have a couple of places to check out. Take a few pictures. You know…the regular stuff…" She trailed off with a shrug, then held her breath when he cupped her breast.

"You have to do it today?" he asked, still frowning and idly stroking his thumb over her nipple.

"Don't forget, I thought you'd be busy working on fences or whatever." She arched against his hand even while telling herself she couldn't afford the distraction. "Did I mention the director is coming tomorrow?"

"Already?"

"Not the film crew. They won't be shooting in Blackfoot Falls until next month. But Jason is coming now."

"What for?"

"He wants to talk to me. He didn't say why."

Spencer lowered his hand and waited for her to look up. "He finally got Moonlight Mountain. He should be pleased about that."

"I haven't told him yet."

"Why not? I signed the agreement. It's not as if I can change my mind."

Erin hesitated, hating herself for even briefly considering she might need it as a bargaining chip. "Yes, you can. That's why I haven't said anything."

"What if that's the reason Jason's coming? Will he stay overnight? Does that mean I won't get to see you tomorrow?"

Erin touched his unshaven cheek, surprised by her shaky hand. His sincerity was so adorably sweet, she wasn't at all prepared for it. "You know what? I don't care about Jason." She meant it. The more she thought about yesterday's cryptic call, the more it irritated her. "He can kiss my butt. Tomorrow night I'm all yours."

Spencer groaned. "Bad image."

She thought for a second and laughed. "Figuratively speaking, of course. Jason? My butt? No," she said, wincing. "Yuck. Definitely not."

"Good to know."

At the possessive gleam in his eye, a shiver raced down her spine. She'd never had a man look at her that way. Had he been anyone else, she wouldn't have liked it. "So, will you come with me today?"

He wrapped his arms around her and pulled her close. "How about we skip the diner? Odds are it'll be too rainy and cold for a picnic. We can come back here and scrape something together."

She smiled up at him. "You have no idea what scraping something together means," she said, shaking her head. "None whatsoever. You eat real food. You even stock your fridge and pantry with grown-up stuff."

"Hey, I went to college. And then veterinary school. I've eaten my share of crap because it was cheap and filling."

"Okay, I believe you." She looped her arms around his neck, trying hard to hold on to a smile.

All that schooling, followed by a minimum one year internship, and then three years residency to become a surgeon… It broke her heart to think he'd given up nearly a third of his life to pursue his passion and then felt he had to just walk away.

His hands skimmed the curve of her butt, and he pulled her against his hot, thick erection. Erin let her head fall back and welcomed his kiss. His tongue pushed past her lips…

What the hell was she doing?

"Wait." She jerked back. "Seriously. We can't do this now. I'm going to miss my appointments."

Spencer frowned at the bedside clock. "Thirty minutes," he said, reeling her back in and nuzzling the side of her neck. "Forty, tops."

"Uh-uh. We both know it won't end—"

He bit her earlobe, then soothed it with his tongue before licking his way down to her nipple.

She almost gave in, but hearing Dusty moving

around down the hall snapped her out of it. "We have plenty of time for this later," she said firmly enough to make him look up.

Slowly he straightened. "You're right. Work first. Play tonight."

"Deal."

Watching him bend down to pick up his towel, she seriously questioned her sanity. They could've spent most of the day in bed, and God only knew she was tempted. With Jason's unexpected arrival tomorrow and then her trip to LA for the awards dinner, she wouldn't have another free day for a while. Which, conveniently or inconveniently, depending on how she chose to look at it, made today the perfect time to take him to Safe Haven. Show him that he didn't have to waste his gift.

She gave his naked ass a final longing look and sighed.

"You can still change your mind," Spencer said, grinning, not even bothering to hide his impressive hard-on. In fact, the way he was holding the towel off to the side…

"Shut up," she said irritably. "And get dressed."

16

"HOW MANY MILES do you have on this thing?" Spencer asked, grimacing when they hit a pothole she hadn't seen in time.

"Sorry," Erin muttered, wishing she'd at least replaced the windshield wipers. The rain was really coming down. "I'll try not to get you killed."

"Sparing both of us would be good."

"You offered to drive. I should've listened." She kept her hands curled around the wheel, her eyes straight ahead, knowing they should be coming up on Safe Haven soon. Yeah, that was stupid not letting him drive. She loved it when he wore his Stetson. She could've stared at him all she wanted.

"With all the driving you do for your job, you need a new car."

"Can't afford it. Maybe next year. Things are looking great for the sequel. So not only will I be the assistant director, I'll actually get paid a salary. How cool is that?"

Spencer chuckled. "You do remember that's how jobs usually work."

"What do you mean? Ranchers don't get salaries,

right? You only get money after you sell your cows. Or something like that."

"Yep, something like that."

He was a terrible passenger. Probably too used to being the one driving. His hand had shot to the dashboard a few times. And he was getting real handy with the *brake* on his side. She figured it was no use assuring him she was a good driver. Hell, she was from LA, where people spent a third of their lives in their cars. Plus, she had no accidents or tickets on her record.

"How does it work running a ranch?" she asked, mostly to distract him. "You have feed to buy, and I assume Dusty gets paid. Obviously budgeting is important. Do you operate off a credit line?" When he didn't answer, she glanced over at him and added, "I'm not being nosy. I meant that as a general question."

"I figured." He shrugged a shoulder. "Finances aren't a problem. Not yet, anyway. My partner had taken out an insurance policy on me. In case I did something stupid," he said with a self-deprecating grunt. "He could've kept the money, sunk it into the practice. Hell, he could've done whatever he wanted. But he gave me all of it. Wished me luck and told me I would always be welcome back to join him."

"He sounds like an amazing person."

Spencer nodded. "I hate that I let him down," he said quietly.

"From how you've described him, I doubt he viewed it that way."

He squinted at the emerging sign up ahead. The rain had eased up, but it was still a bit foggy. "Safe Haven Animal Sanctuary. Is that where we're going?"

"Uh-huh." She could feel his eyes boring into her, but she showed no reaction and concentrated on making a turn onto the gravel road. "I don't know if you've met Shea McAllister—Rachel's sister-in-law. Anyway, Shea volunteers here, and when we were introduced the other day, I told her I'd see if we could use the shelter for a scene in the film. It wouldn't be much money, but something's better than nothing, right?"

He didn't respond, and she resisted the urge to look at him. His silence didn't necessarily mean anything. Since leaving Shadow Creek, there had been periods of heavy rain when they hadn't spoken.

"Looks like a parking lot over to the left," he said, and she couldn't deny the relief she felt that he didn't sound suspicious.

She pulled next to an old white truck loaded with bales of hay covered by a tarp. To their right was a barn. And on her side, a stone walkway led to the office, a cute little log cabin.

Just as they got out of the car, a woman emerged from the barn, bundled up in a parka with tufts of dark hair poking out from under her hood. She was too petite to be Shea. "Good morning. You must be Erin," the woman said, her hand extended. "I'm Kathy, a volunteer here. Shea's been delayed."

"Oh, right, you and Shea are temporarily sharing director duties." Erin shook her hand. "This is Spencer."

"Nice meeting you, ma'am." He reached up to remove his hat. God, she loved seeing him in that Stetson. She was so going to talk him into wearing it to bed tonight.

"Oh, please, don't take off your hat," Kathy said with a wave of her hand, then glanced up at the sky. "The weather's been so strange this year. Earlier we had a horrible downpour." She let her hood drop back and pushed her fingers through her short hair while openly eyeing Spencer. "You must be an actor."

His brows went up. "Me?" He shook his head, looking as if he'd rather be stuck in quicksand than be associated with Hollywood. "No, ma'am. I'm just a simple cowboy."

Erin shot him a wry look and refrained from rolling her eyes.

"Well, you're sure handsome enough to be an actor." She gave Erin a sly wink. "I might not be a young pup anymore, but I can see just fine."

Erin laughed. "You know what? This is the second time he's been mistaken for an actor. I think you're right," she said, giving Spencer a once-over. "He could be a movie star."

"Okay, ladies, you keep talking like that, and I'll have to buy a new hat to fit my head. So, better we change the subject."

Kathy chuckled. "My husband is tending to a sick mare in the quarantine stable," she said, and Erin saw Spencer's jaw tighten. "Levi's been my own personal heartthrob for almost forty years now, so you're plenty safe."

They followed her into the huge barn, and Erin tried to relax by taking deep breaths and counting each one. It was possible her plan could backfire, but she really didn't think so. A quarantine stable? So much better than she could've hoped for. How could Spencer see sick animals and not feel compelled to help them? She continued counting breaths until Kathy turned to her.

"Shea tells me you might be interested in shooting some of your movie here. Is there anything in particular you want to see, or should I give you the regular tour?" Kathy glanced back at the dreary overcast day. "Well, as much as this gloomy weather will allow. I don't wanna get stuck in the mud."

"No," Erin said with a laugh, relieved to see Spencer smile. "Been there, done that." She glanced around the barn at the goats and chickens too busy foraging through the hay-strewn floor to pay them any attention. "What I'd like to do is take some pictures, if you don't mind."

"Not at all. We have the quarantine stable, like I mentioned, another stable where we keep the tack and the horses the volunteers ride. As you can see, the feed is stored in here," Kathy said, gesturing. "We have an equipment shed a ways behind the larger log cabin, which is living quarters. The former director and her husband have been very generous to Safe Haven, so you'll see some new construction mixed with the old."

Nodding, Erin had already taken out her camera and was clicking away. "I noticed you have a lot of corrals. I'm pretty sure we can use some footage there. If not for the current film, maybe for the sequel." She snapped another shot, carefully ignoring Spencer, and said to Kathy, "If you're busy and you don't mind us poking around, we'll be fine on our own."

Kathy seemed to consider the suggestion, then said, "If it was a nice day, I'd take you out on the four-wheelers. We have several acres of alfalfa fields, but there's really nothing to see this time of the year. So how about I take you to the quarantine stable so we don't startle the patients? After that you can just wander as you please. A few volunteers are scattered about, and you can always ask them questions."

Erin smiled. "Perfect." She started to follow Kathy, then realized Spencer was preoccupied with some sort of watering system they'd hooked up to a pair of tanks.

"Wait," Erin stopped when something else occurred to her. "Quarantine? As in isolating infectious viruses? Should I be worried?"

"No." Kathy shook her head. "We don't usually know where the horses are coming from when we take them in. If they show any signs of disease, we have to keep them away from the other horses. It's very rare that a virus can be passed to humans."

"Oh. Good," Erin said, perhaps a bit too quickly. "I'd like to see it."

Spencer looked up, his unsettling lack of expression sending her stomach into a somersault. But then Kathy, noticing his interest, explained how the water tanks were supplied by a central well. No more lugging in heavy buckets of water for the goats and chickens.

By the time they got to the quarantine stable, the two had embarked on yet another conversation about the alfalfa fields a group of local high school kids had planted and were now maintaining.

Kathy introduced them to her husband, Levi, who was tending to a black horse. It broke Erin's heart to see every stall occupied by an ailing animal, and for the first time, she understood this little move of hers could come across as awfully manipulative.

"Spencer bought the old Baker ranch," Kathy was saying to her husband, surprising Erin at first because she hadn't heard him tell Kathy. Then she recalled they'd been talking while she'd detoured to snap a few pictures. "He's donating two truckloads of hay. We just have to let him know when to deliver it."

Levi's eyes widened. "Well, that's real nice of you, son. We've got lots of hungry mouths around here, and I don't have to tell you how expensive hay is..." Levi kept talking, but Erin had stopped listening.

She was too busy studying Spencer's every subtle move. He smiled and nodded at what Levi was saying, but it was clear he was keeping tabs on everything the man was doing to the horse. If she were to quiz Spencer later, she'd bet he had mentally cataloged every medication laid out on the silver tray.

Kathy excused herself with the promise she'd catch up with them later.

Levi gave something to the horse, and Erin asked, "What's wrong with him?"

He smiled fondly at the animal. "Banjo here has what they call parrot mouth or overshot jaw. It's a congenital defect that won't let him process his fodder, so he needs a little extra care is all." He patted the horse's neck. "Makes him prone to digestive disorders. We don't want that, do we, Banjo?"

The horse neighed, and Erin laughed.

"Now, the pair of geldings in the back," Levi said with a sad shake of his head, "they've got equine influenza—basically, it's the flu. But it's highly contagious, so we have to keep them isolated and well rested."

"But they'll be okay, right?"

"I think so. Though there isn't a lot we can do but hope. We're giving them antibiotics, but that's mostly to avoid a secondary infection."

"Are you a vet?" Erin asked, not wanting to look at Spencer, who remained maddeningly silent.

"No." Levi chuckled. "A retired high school teacher. I've been volunteering here some years now, and I've tried to pick up what I can. We only call the vet when we absolutely have to. Doc Yardley's a good man, and he charges us almost nothing, but he's got a family to feed."

Kathy reappeared with a worried frown. "Sorry, folks, I hate to interrupt." She looked at her husband.

"We might have another flu case. It's Buster. Odd, though—he has a thin, gray nasal discharge. I'm not sure where to put him."

"I don't think I've seen that on any of the others." Levi rubbed his eyes and sighed. "I'll come have a look."

"Spencer knows quite a lot about veterinary medicine," Erin said, the words tumbling out of her mouth before she knew it. Risking a glance at him, she saw a wild tic at his jaw.

Levi and Kathy were both looking at Spencer, as well. "Is that so?" Levi asked. "I certainly wouldn't mind a more educated opinion."

Spencer hesitated. "Has he been coughing?" he finally asked. "Even occasionally?"

Kathy's face reddened. "I'm not sure. We have so many horses to look after..."

"Of course." Spencer nodded and gave her a kind smile. "I understand. Where do you keep him? The corrals? The stable?"

"The stable," Levi said and moved to put an arm around his wife. "Another volunteer and I usually ride him to the pastures."

"It's possible he's suffering from COPD, basically the equine equivalent to asthma. He could be having an allergic reaction to fungal spores in the hay or straw." Spencer shrugged. "But that's just a guess. I could be completely wrong."

"If that were the case, what should we be doing?" Levi asked.

After a long stretch of awkward silence, with Spencer clenching and unclenching his jaw, he said, "Look, I'd hate to steer you in the wrong direction."

Kathy looked helplessly at Levi, who was studying

Spencer. "I don't see we have much choice but to call Doc Yardley," Kathy said softly.

"Erin?" Spencer's mask was back in place. "Let's go. We don't need to be taking up their time right now."

She wanted to argue. She wanted to scream at him to at least have a look at the horse. Kathy was obviously upset. Levi, too, but he was better at hiding it. How could Spencer just leave? Finally, Erin swallowed and nodded.

"I'm so sorry about this," Kathy said as Levi started walking. "You can still wander about if you want."

"Don't worry about us." Erin waved her on. "Go. We'll talk later."

Kathy nodded and hurried to catch up with Levi.

Spencer didn't say a word as he led them to the parking lot. He opened the driver's door for her but didn't wait to close it. Sliding onto the passenger seat, he yanked off his hat when it bumped the ceiling.

He waited until she'd buckled herself in and put the key in the ignition, then said in a low, furious voice, "What the hell was that, Erin?"

She blinked at him. The anger in his face knocked the wind out of her. She forced herself to put the car in gear and drive out of the parking lot. They had to talk, but it couldn't be here.

SPENCER HELD BACK while she drove down the gravel road to the highway. It wasn't easy. He couldn't remember the last time he'd been this infuriated. He drew in air, waiting, expecting that she'd pull over as soon as it was safe. At least he hoped that was her plan, because he wouldn't last much longer without exploding.

The thing was, Erin was smart. She had to know he'd see right through this trumped-up trip to Safe Haven.

Although he'd admit that she'd had him fooled in the beginning. Wanting to film at the sanctuary wasn't such a reach.

After driving about a mile on the highway she pulled off at a small turnout and cut the engine. He noticed her hand tremble as she lowered it from the steering wheel.

"I'm sorry I mentioned anything about you," she said. "It just came out."

He waited for her to look at him. "Is that it?"

She frowned slightly. "I don't remember saying anything else that you would object to…"

"Why Safe Haven? Why bring me out here?"

"You know why. I came to check out the place and take pictures."

Spencer shook his head, itching to punch something. He flexed his hand. "That's all? You had no other reason to bring me with you. Today. Of all days."

"Oh, please. How could I have known it was going to rain and you'd have a free day?" She averted her eyes and stared out the windshield. "But you're right," she said softly, turning back to meet his gaze. "The rain was pure luck. I wanted you to see Safe Haven. I'd hoped it would help you see how incredibly useful you can be. And still do what you love—"

"Stop."

"Can I just finish?"

"You think I haven't heard all of this before? Jesus. I told you why I left Boise."

"I get it. I do. But it's been almost a year since the accident, and maybe if you'd just give yourself—"

"It wasn't an accident. I played with fire, and I got burned. My fault. I've never denied that. So don't say you get it, because you don't." Spencer felt hemmed in. He hated small cars. Hated being a passenger. Hell, he'd walk back to Shadow Creek if it weren't so damn far. Shit. Why had he told her about his past? Another dumb move.

"Can I say one more thing?"

Sighing, Spencer briefly closed his eyes. "Leave it alone, Erin. Please." He looked into her determined face and knew she wasn't about to back off. Didn't she understand she was ripping open an old wound? One he'd fought hard to mend. He had to end this. Anger was churning inside him, looking for release, and right now, he didn't trust himself. "Let me ask you something first."

She nodded, closely studying his features, making him feel raw and naked. And weak.

He felt like a goddamn loser.

"What is it that makes you think you have the right to interfere in my life?" He held her gaze steady, even after her slight flinch. "Is it because we had sex?" He waited. "Huh? Is that it?"

She bit her lip and kept staring at him.

"Great sex, I'll grant you that," he continued. "But you're a smart woman, Erin, and I can't see how you would've interpreted it as permission to stick your nose in my business. Especially when you damn well know how much I value my privacy."

"I'm not— I— If only you'd seen your face after you stitched me up, then you'd understand—"

He held up a hand. "Look, I admire you and how you're going after your dream with everything you have. Please, respect the fact that I knew when to walk away."

Despite everything, the disappointment in her eyes turned the knife in his chest another fifty degrees.

"There's nothing more to talk about," he said. "Let's get on the road."

17

After a fitful night's sleep, Erin forced herself out of bed. The first thing she did was check her phone. She knew Spencer hadn't called or texted, because she would've heard it. Not that she'd expected him to call. Certainly not last night. Or today. Or probably ever. He'd been so angry when she'd dropped him off yesterday.

He hadn't shouted or cussed or any of those things. But the low pitch of despair in his voice had been ten times worse. If only he'd heard her out. She'd truly wanted to help. He was right, though. It was none of her business. What he needed was a little more time to come to the same conclusion she had—that he wasn't finished.

She took her phone with her into the bathroom. The way her luck was running, she'd hear from Jason that he was already here. He was due to arrive midafternoon, and she didn't need him moving up the time. She still had to get her act together.

The minute she stepped out of the shower she heard Lila's ringtone. Erin grabbed a towel, then her cell.

"Hey," she said and waited to be sure it was Lila and not Jason pulling another fast one.

"Yeah, it's me."

"Could you hold on a sec?" Erin hastily dried herself and then pulled her nightshirt back on, hoping Lila could give her a heads-up on Jason's visit. "So, did you find out anything?"

"Sort of… Jason found an investor."

"Now? For this project?"

"I think so."

"What do you mean, you think? He can't take outside money without telling the rest of us first. Don't we all have to vote or at least agree?"

"I'm not sure that's true. He used the money from his inheritance to put in the most capital. He might have discussed it with David and Brian because they invested that chunk, as well, but you and I are at the bottom of the totem pole."

"Yeah, but you and I used up all our savings, took out loans, and we're working for nothing." Erin walked into the bedroom and sat on the bed. "Maybe that's why he's coming here today. To tell me in person."

"That's the only reason I can think of. And honestly, it may not be a bad move. This backer supposedly has pretty deep pockets, and word is, the sequel is a done deal. So don't be too pissed at him, okay?"

Erin rubbed her eyes. Assuming that was all true, it meant she would officially be named first AD. "Yeah, but there's got to be a catch. Hell, that's the name of the game. That's why we didn't want to take outside money in the first place. Dammit. I'm too exhausted to talk to him today…"

"Well, that's what you get for canoodling with lover boy all night."

Erin sighed. "I wish."

After a short silence, Lila said, "Erin? What's going on?"

"I screwed up with Spencer."

"How?"

"By being me." She said it as a joke, but sadly, the remark was all too true. "You know what? This really isn't the time to talk about it. I've got Jason coming and I…" Her gaze fell on the envelope containing the contract.

"Darn it, Erin. You can't leave me hanging. You know how much I hate that."

Erin smiled. *Darn it* was strong language for Lila.

"Does it have to do with Moonlight Mountain?"

"No. Spencer signed the agreement, but I just decided I'm not giving it to Jason."

"Are you insane?"

"Probably." Shit. She wanted to scream. Kick something. Cry her eyes out. But none of those things would help. Instead, she briefly explained what had happened after Safe Haven.

"That's not so terrible," Lila said. "I bet it blows over."

"I want to believe that, but God, Lila, you didn't see his face. He was so angry and hurt and…" *Disappointed.* That hadn't registered until just now. And she really wished it hadn't.

"Have you talked to him since yesterday?"

"No," Erin said, checking the time. "And, no, I didn't try calling him, either."

"You know what I think?"

Oh, Jesus. She loved Lila like a sister. More than a sister. But Erin knew what was coming, and she couldn't take it right now. "Don't go getting all Pollyanna on me. You know I hate that shit."

Lila sniffed. "I was only going to suggest you invite him to the awards dinner next week."

"Did you not hear anything I said?"

"Well, of course you should apologize first, then tell him about the big award you're definitely receiving, maybe even two, and how you'd like him to be there with you."

Erin wasn't sure how to respond. "Now who's insane?"

"Look, from everything you've told me about Spencer, he sounds like a great guy, and, yeah, he might be pissed, but when things calm down, he'll figure out you meant well. It wasn't like you outed him."

No, she'd done far worse. The day Spencer had taken care of her gash, he'd told her he wasn't willing to discuss why he'd quit practicing, and she'd agreed. Practically promised him she'd stay out of his business. Yesterday she'd broken that promise. Her intentions didn't mean crap.

"Erin?"

"Still here. Just thinking about what you said."

Lila laughed softly. "Baloney. But I wish you would. Spencer might surprise you." Lila paused. "Do you think he'll renege on Moonlight Mountain?"

"No, he wouldn't do that." Spencer wasn't the type of man to go back on his word. He wasn't like Erin. She swallowed her disappointment. "I gave Jason a couple of excellent alternatives. It's not as if I'm leaving him high and dry."

When Lila didn't respond, Erin said, "I have to go. I don't know when to expect him, so I'd better go do something with this hair."

"Call me later," Lila said. "After you talk to Jason.

Oh, and cheer up, for goodness' sake. You're going to be an AD!"

Erin managed a little smile. "Let's not get too excited until after the ink dries."

TWO HOURS LATER Erin met Jason in the inn's tiny lobby.

He wore his customary faded jeans, but the blue designer shirt was new and not at all typical. And the expensive-looking black leather jacket?

"Somebody splurged," she said, eyeing him up and down. Damn, nice boots, too. All courtesy of the new investor, she wondered.

"Yeah." He tugged at the front of the jacket. "It gets colder than shit around here," he said and leaned in to kiss her cheek.

Surprised, she took half a step back. What the hell was that about? "Are we just talking, or did you want a brief tour of the area?"

"Both. Mostly talking, though. How about your room? Can we talk there?"

"The diner might be better. My room is really small."

Jason nodded thoughtfully. "Yeah, okay. I think the diner would be better, anyway."

"We can walk." She glanced toward the window. The sky was blue and the sun was out. "It's about four blocks."

He shook his head, and she saw that he'd tied his sandy-blond hair back into a short ponytail. "Let's drive. We'll take my car."

"Fine." She patted her jeans pocket, making sure she had her phone and room key as they left the lobby.

Something was off with him. He'd been keyed up for months, and this new calm made her edgy. Maybe he was more relaxed because of the recent influx of cash.

Other than her pointing out a couple of storefronts, the short ride was silent. Several people greeted her on the street and in the diner, and stared at Jason with open curiosity.

He gestured for her to choose a booth. Perversely she went straight for the corner table she'd shared with Spencer only a week ago.

After they both ordered coffee, Jason studied her across the table. "I'm sure you've heard about the new investor."

"I heard." She shrugged a shoulder. "I figured you were here to lobby for my vote in person."

"Your vote?"

"We all agreed on a ceiling for investors. To make sure we maintained control of the project." She watched his face cloud over. "I'm assuming this new person is offering much more than the amount we set."

"We're not voting on anything. I don't even know where you got that idea."

"If you're proposing to change the rules, don't we all have to agree? What did David and Brian have to say? We all have a stake in this movie."

"They're both fine with it. Mostly because we don't have a choice. Hell, it looks as if we'll be filming all the way until January. We hadn't planned on that. Do you know how damn lucky we are that someone was willing to write us a check?"

Erin sighed. "You already have the money." She'd figured as much, but it still sucked. "It's a done deal."

His wary expression was confirmation enough.

Neither of them spoke as a waitress Erin didn't recognize set down their coffee.

She smiled her thanks, then picked up her mug and took a sip. "Oh, shit."

Hot. Really hot.

Jason laughed. "You do that all the time. When are you gonna learn?"

"Shut up." She laughed along with him. Why was she giving him a hard time? In truth, she was probably less surprised than Jason that their finances hadn't held up. They'd all been starry-eyed from the start, willing to bet everything. "Okay, for the record, I still don't like that you didn't ask if we had any objections, but I understand."

He looked somewhat relieved. But something else was bothering him.

Her chest tightened instinctively. "Of course there's a catch. Always is when it comes to money. So what is it?"

"Listen, Erin," he said, exhaling long and hard. "This isn't easy for me to say..."

She watched the nervous bob of his Adam's apple, and her tummy cramped in response. "What?" She kept her voice low, suddenly wishing they had gone to the privacy of her room. "Dammit, just tell me!"

"This new investor...Paul Mortimer, he's got a lot of money, Erin, and he doesn't mind dishing it out." Jason leaned forward, excitement glittering in his eyes. "He'll give us whatever we need for the sequel. In writing. Right now. It wouldn't matter how this film is received by the public or the critics..." He inhaled and leaned back. "But only if I make his nephew first AD."

"What? Who the hell is this guy? He can't do that." Seeing the guilt and sympathy in Jason's eyes, she felt sick to her stomach. "Did you tell him we already have a first assistant director?" She pushed the mug aside, the smell of coffee no longer agreeing with her. "Huh, Jason? Did you explain to him that I gave up my life, my savings...everything. So I could be AD?"

"See, Erin, that's the thing. We're flush. I can even pay you a retroactive salary…it won't be a lot but something to help—or what about the loan you took out? What if I could pay it off?"

Heat surged up her throat and stung her cheeks. She couldn't imagine how red her face was. By the look of alarm in Jason's eyes, she was guessing it was pretty bad.

"Look," he said, "it's just a temporary setback. The kid doesn't know shit about filmmaking. I'll name you as second AD, but you'll be calling the shots, I promise."

"Yeah, because your promises mean so damn much. So what? I do all the work, and this kid gets all the credit?"

He flinched. "I know you're upset. And I don't blame—"

"Ya think?" She had to calm down. People were beginning to stare. "Pay off the loan? Give me a salary? You know damn well it's not about money."

"But this gives us even more cachet for next time—"

"Us?" She shook her head, both angry and sad at the same time. "Jason, do you remember back in school, sitting around, talking about Hollywood and how we were going to stick together? No backstabbing, no—"

"Come on, that's not fair."

"Don't talk to me about fair."

"Hey, I have a lot of money invested in this, myself. More than the rest of you put together."

"You're absolutely right. We were lucky you'd received that inheritance money. But that still isn't the point, is it, Jason?"

Perfectly aware of how much of herself she'd poured into the project, he averted his gaze.

God, she was tired. Exhausted. Not because she hadn't slept much. It felt as though she'd been treading water forever just to keep the dream alive. And she was no closer to her goal than she'd been a year ago.

"Look, Erin, I dreaded having to tell you this, but at least I had the balls to do it in person." He waited expectantly—for a clap on the back or a thank-you? Who the hell knew? "Hey, how about we get a drink at one of the bars? Talk a little about the last scene. I really want your input. I need you, kiddo," he said with a resigned smile. "We both know that."

She knew he wasn't patronizing her. Jason really did need her. She was very good at many different things, and she pushed harder than anyone else to get the job done. That was exactly why she was up for two AFI awards next week. The American Film Institute recognized hard work and achievement. She felt honored just to be nominated.

But now she felt defeated. Devoid of hope. The film industry was never going to change. Money and power would always win. But sadly, her friend had changed, and that was what drained the fight out of her.

"Erin, you're too quiet. You're making me nervous."

She huffed a laugh. "Who knows about the nephew?"

"No one."

"Not Brian or David?"

He shook his head. "I wanted to tell you first."

"Good. Lila can't know. Not yet." Erin gave him a death stare. "You promised Lila a juicy role. You screw her out of that, and I'll walk. Do you understand?"

Jason nodded slowly. A sheen of sweat coated his forehead. He knew it wasn't an idle threat. "Lila will be taken care of. Can you give me your assurance you'll stay for the sequel?" Met with silence, a nervous smile tugged at his mouth. "I'll get down on my knees and beg right here if that's what you want."

She looked at him, tempted to put him through the wringer. But she didn't have the energy. "You already gave away the only thing I wanted," she said and slid out of the booth.

He had the good grace to blush. "Where are you going?"

"To pack." She enjoyed the flicker of panic in his eyes before she added, "I have the awards dinner next weekend. I may as well head back to LA."

He dug out cash and threw it on the table. "I kind of hate to ask, but…what about Moonlight Mountain?"

"Not gonna happen." She glanced around at the nosy stares. "I don't need a ride back to the inn. I'd rather walk."

Jason was about to argue, but she told him with a look it would be a bad move.

"You'll be in touch?" he asked.

She nodded and hurried out of the diner without stopping to talk to anyone. Thank God for the awards ceremony. It was the perfect excuse to get the hell out of Blackfoot Falls. Not that she felt like going to the dinner anymore. She was done with all of that bullshit. The dream had been so much better than the reality. Time to wake up. Do something useful with her life.

Right now, though, her only goal was to find some peace and quiet. Some solitude where no one could get in her face. She hadn't been home in three months, and the timing was perfect, since she'd have the apartment to herself. Lila would be tied up here until shooting wrapped up.

Yes, getting on the road as quickly as possible would be her best move. After all, there was nothing left for her here, not after she'd screwed up so royally with Spencer.

She almost stopped right where she stood, halfway down Main Street, cars driving past her, people giving her friendly waves that barely registered. How had it taken her so long to see she'd been living in an illusion? How many *next times* would she be willing to accept to make it to the big league?

She'd seen people all around her fold—talented people with drive and ambition who'd been used up and cast aside. Yes, a few made it to the top. A very few. But at what cost?

This wasn't the first time Jason or someone else on the rise had promised her something without delivering. She didn't believe it was intentional on his part. They'd worked well together on other projects, and she knew he valued her talent. But when it came down to the wire, she was expendable.

Spencer had the guts and good sense to walk away when his dream had fallen apart.

She finally understood the courage it had taken for him to make such a difficult decision. He hadn't wimped out. He'd chosen to change course. She'd been playing at this business for far too long, taking what she could get instead of deciding what she needed. Hell, she should have done this so differently. At least had a plan B. But she'd been blinded by the stars in her eyes while her life passed her by. And she felt so utterly ashamed.

18

SPENCER STOOD AT the counter staring at the coffeepot trying to recall why he'd come into the kitchen. The empty mug in his hand finally tipped him off.

Muttering a curse, he glanced at his phone, sitting near the stove where he'd left it earlier. Still nothing from Erin. Last he'd heard from her was a text five days ago. Telling him she was on her way to LA and that she'd left the signed agreement for Moonlight Mountain at the inn's front desk.

Dusty had picked up the envelope for him. The contract had been torn in half. Along with it she'd included a note advising him it would be a mistake to grant access to anyone from Hollywood. That was it. No other texts or calls, even though he'd left a voice mail two days ago.

He wanted to talk to her. Admit that she'd been right. Not that he agreed with her methods. But he'd done some serious soul-searching and decided he wasn't ready to give up on himself, on all the education and training he'd received, or on the potential he had yet to explore. He'd even been in touch with Levi about the gelding with COPD. Turned out the local vet concurred with Spencer's suspicion and the animal was on the mend.

Levi had joked about wishing he'd listened to Spencer and saved Safe Haven an unnecessary bill. Spencer hadn't hesitated. He'd set up a time to meet with Levi and Kathy. While he still wasn't sure how much he wanted them to know or even what he was prepared to offer, he was more than willing to help out at the sanctuary. Hell, he looked forward to it.

And dammit, he wanted to tell Erin. But not by leaving a voice mail. The thought he might never see her again worried him. If she returned to Blackfoot Falls to work on the film, that didn't necessarily mean she'd want to see him. She thought he was a quitter. Something a strong-willed woman like Erin could never understand or respect.

Spencer thought he heard a car door. Dusty was in the stable, so Spencer moved to the window just as a tall blonde got out of a silver compact.

The woman glanced around before heading toward the house. Spencer's chest tightened. He'd never seen a picture of Lila, but for some reason he knew it was her.

He opened the door after her first knock.

Big blue eyes stared at him. "Spencer Hunt?"

Nodding, he said, "Lila?"

She seemed only mildly surprised he knew who she was. He gestured for her to come inside, and she entered the house.

"May I take your coat?"

"No, thanks. I'm not staying long." She flashed him a smile. She was a beauty, just as Erin had claimed.

"Have you talked to Erin?" they both asked at the same time.

"No," Spencer said, noting the woman's worried

frown. She was shivering, so he led her into the kitchen to get her something hot to drink. "Evidently you haven't, either."

"Not for three days."

"I got a text the day she left, and that's it." He held up the pot of coffee, and she nodded. A bad feeling swept over him. He'd gotten the impression the two talked just about every day.

"I'm worried about her," Lila said, accepting a mug and spooning in sugar. A *lot* of sugar. "This is what I do when I'm stressed. I live on sweets. Not great for an actress. Erin knows that. So as soon as I find her, I'm going to kill her."

"She's *missing*?"

"No. I said that wrong. She just isn't answering her phone, and I don't know why. Not for sure, anyway." Lila took a quick breath. "Have you spoken to her at all since that day she took you to the animal sanctuary?"

Naturally Erin would've told her friend about that. And about him. He tightened his mouth and shook his head.

"The next day she had a meeting with Jason. The director. I'm sure Erin told you she's in line to be the assistant director for the next film. It's a huge deal, and Erin totally deserves the position. But I'm afraid Jason has pulled a fast one so he could get money from an investor. Meaning he might've reneged on Erin. That's why he wanted to speak to her privately." Anger flared in Lila's eyes, and she turned away with a dainty sniffle. "Erin denied it. She said we're both safe and she's just angry about him taking money without consulting us. But that can't be all of it, and now she's ducking my calls."

Spencer's thoughts were splintering off in all directions.

He knew how much she'd been counting on the AD job. "No wonder she tore up the agreement," he murmured, more to himself.

"No, she did that before she talked to Jason."

"How do you know?"

"Because she told me that morning. I thought she was crazy." Lila sighed. "It isn't even like her to get sentimental," she said and started pacing. "Our last call, she sounded kind of down, but I figured she was tired from the long drive. But it's more than— I think she's finally had enough. She's giving up."

"What do you mean giving up?"

"It's just… Her work is just beginning to be recognized. She's about to get this big AFI award on Saturday. Possibly two awards. You probably know she produced a short, as well as a documentary, and everyone was totally blown away. But it's been such an uphill battle. One step forward, four steps back. And then Jason selling out…"

Lila was still talking, but Spencer heard very little. He was too stunned that Erin hadn't told him about the awards. Sure, he knew about the dinner, but she hadn't mentioned one word about being a nominee.

And that surprised him? Erin was all about the integrity of the work and the pure joy of creating. She wasn't doing it for awards or accolades. While he'd truly loved his job, he couldn't deny he'd also enjoyed the attention of being the hotshot "brilliant" new surgeon.

Erin hadn't judged him for throwing away his career by being a fool. She'd only wanted him to see that he didn't have to give up his whole dream.

"Are you serious about her giving up? Because that doesn't sound like her."

"I know," Lila said, throwing up her hands. "Why do you think I'm so worried?"

He flexed his hand and studied the fading scar. Erin had seen right through him and stepped up to show him the way. He couldn't stand the thought of her feeling whipped and defeated. Not Erin.

"Just so you know, she doesn't have a date for the dinner."

He looked up. Lila had stopped pacing and was staring at him.

"Just so I know?"

Lila smiled. "We share an apartment in Santa Clarita." She took a piece of paper out of her coat pocket and passed it to him. "Here's the address. In case you happen to be in the neighborhood," she said and started for the door. "Oh, and dinner is black-tie."

Spencer grunted. Jesus. California women were something else. He followed her to the door and, after he closed it, went to the window.

"Holy shit!" Dusty appeared out of nowhere and watched Lila walk to her car. "I think I'm in love."

"Don't do it, kid," Spencer said, sighing. "Love hurts like hell."

ERIN HAD CLOSED all the windows and dug out a space heater from the storage closet when she first got home. But a week later the apartment still felt chilly. The cold tile underneath the old rug she was sitting on didn't help. It didn't matter. She didn't have the energy to move.

She taped up another box of books. Some of them were fiction, but mostly they were her old textbooks from college. She really didn't need them anymore, but she wasn't quite ready to donate them to the library yet.

Or maybe she should have a giant bonfire. A symbol that she was officially over her whole moviemaking obsession. Lila would help; she'd be all over it. They could do it on the beach. Spread blankets on the sand like they'd done back in high school. Bring pizza and beer, invite some friends.

She was liking the idea more and more. A bonfire would be highly dramatic and totally fitting.

Erin sighed. Hell, she didn't know if Lila was even speaking to her at this point. Although Erin had finally replied to her texts, she couldn't trust herself to have a conversation that wouldn't blow up in her face.

Erin wasn't an actress. She'd never be able to fool Lila, who knew her better than anyone else on earth. Besides, Erin had used up all of her excuses—too busy looking for a dress for the dinner, misplaced her phone, forgot to charge it…

Normally, Jason and his bullshit would be exactly the kind of thing the two of them would talk about. But this was different. Lila's dream was still intact, and Erin would never, no matter what happened, do or say anything that would burst Lila's bubble. The role she'd been promised in the sequel would get her noticed big-time. Lila wasn't just a pretty face; she was a damn good actress. She'd studied her craft and took it seriously. A showcase was all she needed.

And as for Spencer—

God.

How could thinking about him still hurt so much?

He was a good man. Of course he'd forgiven her by now. Hopefully because he knew she hadn't meant any harm. Misguided? Stubborn? Single-minded? Yes to all of those things. But she wasn't cruel or a bully. Even though she might've come across that way.

Several days earlier, he'd left her a voice mail, and she owed him a response. But it would have to be later, when she could be certain she wouldn't make more of a mess of whatever fragile relationship they had left.

She hadn't set her hopes too high.

Someone knocked at the door.

Erin looked up but ignored it like always. Ten to one it was a food delivery for her neighbor. When Gabbie got stoned, she ordered pizza or Chinese and often gave the restaurant the wrong apartment number.

Shit. Chinese sounded good.

Erin jumped up. If this was one of those times, screw it. She'd keep the order.

Hungry for the first time in days, she grabbed her wallet on the way to the door. She pulled it open and stared in shock. Okay, this couldn't be good. If he was a hallucination, why the hell would he be wearing a tux?

Spencer looked at her ratty T-shirt and torn jeans. "Why aren't you ready? Dinner is in three hours. And man, the traffic around here sucks."

Erin shook her head. "What are you doing here?"

"I'm your date."

"Let me guess. Lila?"

"She's worried about you," he said, and Erin's chest tightened. "So am I."

"Get in here. My neighbors will think you're a stripper."

He glanced at her wallet. "Were you expecting one? Do I get a tip?"

"You do look pretty hot," she said, eyeing him as he walked past her, hoping she sounded normal. Because, crap, tight chest, pounding heart. Not a great combination.

Spencer glanced around the small living room with more boxes than furniture. He met her gaze. "I understand you're set to receive a big award. Why aren't you dressed?"

"They'll send it to me." Erin tossed her wallet on the couch and turned to a bookshelf crammed with DVDs. How could he be standing three feet from her? It wasn't possible. "I got your voice mail, and I was planning on calling…"

He waited for her to look at him again. "But?"

"I didn't know what to say."

Spencer choked out a laugh. "You expect me to believe that?"

Erin smiled a little. "I'm trying to actually think before I speak. See how that works out for me."

The humor left his face. "Don't skip the dinner."

"There's no point in going. I'm finished with Hollywood," she said and caught herself. "Look, you can't tell Lila. About me quitting. Or anything we talk about." Erin paused. "What did she tell you?"

"She thinks Jason might've reneged on the assistant director's position."

"But he didn't tell Lila that, right?" She waited for Spencer to nod. "Part of our deal is he keeps his mouth shut and Lila gets her shot. I'll head back to Blackfoot Falls for the wrap-up and go wherever they need me for the sequel. Lila has a lot riding on this film, and I won't disappoint her. But after that, I'm done."

"I don't believe it."

Sighing, Erin shoved both hands through her hair. She realized then she had to look like shit. She hadn't brushed her hair in days. Thank God she'd at least brushed her teeth.

She looked at him, so suave and handsome in the crisp white shirt and black tux, and she smiled. "You're gorgeous."

"So are you." He took her hand and pulled her closer. "What you aren't is a quitter."

"I used to think that," she said, "and honestly, I don't see myself as a quitter, but I am done. You were right to walk away, and I feel like such an idiot. I had no business trying to push you back into something you didn't want to do."

"No, it wasn't any of your business, but you did help me see some things I hadn't been ready to deal with after the accident. I'm not done with veterinary medicine, just like you aren't done with Hollywood. It's in your blood. Even I can see that." He ignored her condescending smile and kissed her.

"As two arguably intelligent people," he continued, the corners of his mouth twitching, "we'll have to adapt. Instead of mourning the chances we missed, go for the dream that's possible." His brows went up. "Don't give me that cynical look. You taught me that. And now you'd better be thinking about heeding the same advice you gave me."

Again, she didn't know what to say. She had to think about this.

"Question," he said, stroking the side of her arm. "Is making a documentary much different than making a movie?"

She laughed. "Um, yeah, a little bit."

"But you've produced documentaries, and you might be getting an award for it."

"True."

"Documentaries are often controversial. I imagine you'd be all over that."

"Again, true." She narrowed her gaze. "Where are you going with this?"

"Remember the conversation I had with Matt Gunderson about cloning American quarter horses?"

"Sort of."

"Whether or not clones should be allowed to be registered is a pretty hot topic."

"Are you trying to lure me into something?"

Spencer grinned. "Definitely. And after that, we can talk about documentaries again."

She laughed. "I thought you hated me."

"I didn't hate you. I hated myself. Here you were fighting for what you wanted. I'd had everything I'd dreamed of, and I blithely walked away like a spoiled, selfish prick."

"No. It was me. I had no right to interfere—"

"Look, Erin, I knew the moment I told you about what happened, you wouldn't be content to back off. You don't give up. And I don't want to see you throw in the towel now. And, yes, I'm interfering. Tough."

She studied him for a moment. "I'm not going to the dinner," she said and put her arms around his waist. "If I'm getting the award, it'll happen whether I'm there or not." She jerked his shirt from his trousers. "And as hot as you look in this tux, I'm more interested in what you have underneath."

Spencer smiled.

"So," she continued, "I suggest we get horizontal and then—" She let out a squeal when he picked her up and set her on the counter separating the kitchen and living room. "Or not."

He pulled up her T-shirt, smiled at her pink bra.

"Nice," he murmured and nibbled her through the lacy cup.

Her arms got tangled for a moment, but then she flung the T-shirt across the room before attacking his jacket and shirt. The cummerbund almost defeated her.

"Damn, tuxedos are a pain in the ass."

Spencer put his arms around her and smiled. "I have faith in you."

"Oh, I'll get you naked," she promised, but stopped at the warm look on his face. "I have faith in you, too," she whispered.

He rested his forehead against hers. "We're good together, Erin."

She wouldn't nod because she didn't want to break contact. But she couldn't speak, either. Finally, she took his face in her hands and smiled through a sheen of tears. "Bet you thought you were rid of me."

"No." He leaned back and unfastened the cummerbund, then unzipped her jeans. "I thought I blew it. This time I won't be walking away. I'd lose too much."

Erin wanted to second the motion. But she still couldn't speak, so she kissed him instead.

* * * * *

COMING NEXT MONTH FROM

Available August 23, 2016

#907 HANDLE ME

Uniformly Hot!

by Kira Sinclair

Military K-9 handler Ty Colson has been lusting after his best friend's little sister for years. Now she's finally letting him into her bed, but will she ever let him into her heart?

#908 TEMPTED IN THE CITY

NYC Bachelors

by Jo Leigh

Tony Paladino is a licensed contractor who is Little Italy royalty. Catherine Fox hires Tony to renovate her downtown property. The attraction is fierce—and mutual. Too bad they're complete opposites!

#909 HOT SEDUCTION

Hotshot Heroes

by Lisa Childs

Serena Beaumont has always been the good girl, the one who wants a husband and kids. But when she rents a room to a notorious player, Hotshot firefighter Cody Mallehan, she's tempted to be very, *very* bad.

#910 NO LIMITS

Space Cowboys

by Katherine Garbera

Astronaut Jason "Ace" McCoy wasn't expecting to add *rancher* to his job title. Will a few sizzling weeks with his ranch co-owner, Molly Tanner, tempt him to give up the stars and stay in the saddle for good?

SPECIAL EXCERPT FROM

HARLEQUIN® *Blaze®*

When military K-9 handler Ty Colson delivers retired war dog Kaia to her new owner, Van Cantrell's head wants nothing to do with the risk-hungry soldier determined to return to the front lines. But her body has other ideas…

Read on for a sneak preview of HANDLE ME, the first of Kira Sinclair's ***UNIFORMLY HOT!*** *K-9 stories.*

"I suggest you do exactly what I plan on doing and forget that night ever happened."

Van stared out at the neighborhood she called home. It was quiet. Nice. Full of professionals and families. She wanted to like it here, but honestly, it had never quite felt like home.

She felt him way before she heard him. All that pent-up tension and heat slipping over her skin like fingers, caressing her into a reaction she didn't want to feel.

Ty didn't actually touch her, though. He didn't have to.

"You keep telling yourself that, princess," he whispered, the soft puff of his breath tickling her ear. A shiver rolled down her spine. He was too close not to notice.

He chuckled.

Van ground her teeth together, though she wasn't sure if it was to bite back words or merely find another—safer—outlet for all that pent-up energy.

"I remember every moment of that night," he

HBEXP0816

murmured, his words low and dangerous to her equilibrium.

"Highly unlikely considering how drunk you were."

His fingertips found the curve of her neck and slowly, devastatingly trailed across her skin. Goose bumps erupted in the wake of his touch, a telltale sign she was powerless to hide.

"I stopped drinking the minute we hit that tree house. I was sober as a judge by the time things got…heated."

"Ha!"

"The way you looked, naked, flushed with desire and spread out on that blanket, is something I'll never forget. Not as long as I live." Ty swept her hair over one shoulder, exposing the curve of her neck. The warm summer breeze ghosted over her, replaced almost immediately by the blazing heat of his mouth.

She whimpered. The sound simply escaped, uncontrollable and way too revealing.

No. "I can't do this," she said, the words coming out a strangled mess. "You're the reason my brother is dead. He never should have been in Afghanistan. He followed *you* into that life. My body might think you're God's gift to continuing the species, but my brain doesn't give a shit."

Ty's gaze hardened, his eyes like ice. In that moment she could see the ruthless, fearless, dangerous soldier that he'd become. "Take Kaia inside and be sure to give her plenty of water." His voice was flat. "I'll be back tomorrow."

Love the Harlequin book you just read?

Your opinion matters.

Review this book on your favorite book site, review site, blog or your own social media properties and share your opinion with other readers!